About

Alan Gorevan is an award-winning writer and intellectual property attorney. He lives in Dublin. Visit his website at www.alangorevan.com

By Alan Gorevan

The Forbidden Room
The Hostage
Hit and Run

Hit and Run

Alan Gorevan

Copyright © 2020 by Alan Gorevan

All rights reserved

No part of this book may be reproduced, stored in a retrieval system or transmitted by any means without the written permission of the author.

This book is a work of fiction. People, places, events and situations are the product of the author's imagination. Any resemblance to actual persons, living or dead, or historical events, is purely coincidental.

ISBN: 9798643954439

HIT AND RUN

CHAPTER ONE

I'm dying, Jake Whelan thought.

He had only climbed one flight of stairs, but his suit felt tight and his lungs screamed for air. Maybe this was how a heart attack felt.

He pushed himself to continue, up one more flight of stairs.

On the fifth floor, Jake stopped and leaned against the wall. He still felt like he was dying, but it was probably all in his head. Climbing a couple of dozen steps shouldn't kill a healthy thirty-two-year-old. He was a healthy weight and suffered from no underlying health condition.

The smell in the stairwell was unpleasant – like new carpet – but Jake was glad he hadn't taken the elevator. Confined spaces were murder these days.

He pushed open the door and set off down the fifth-floor corridor.

"Hey, handsome."

Liz Dubois was coming from the bank of elevators. His girlfriend of a year wore a long golden skirt and a green blouse which complemented her flowing brown hair. She adjusted her glasses, and said, "You weren't in your office. I thought I'd catch you here."

Jake took a breath.

"You scared the hell out of me," he said.

Liz frowned. "I don't know why you're so jumpy."

He took the envelope she held out to him. A *Good Luck* card was inside. In careful, curly letters, Liz had written, *To Jake, my partner.* She'd doodled a cartoon heart next to her signature.

Jake forced a smile. "Thanks, Liz."

She threw her arms around him, squeezing him so tight that it hurt.

"I just wanted to wish you luck. I know you don't need it. I'm sure you'll get the promotion."

As always, Liz's words were clipped and precise, her accent the product of a French father and a German mother.

"How's your dad?" Jake asked, pulling away from her.

"His aide says he's in good spirits."

Wednesday nights, Liz had her weekly teleconference with her father. Christian Dubois had lived in the Grüne Felder private hospital in Munich for years, battling ALS. He was almost completely paralysed and could only communicate now by blinking. Fortunately, his aide was a French-speaker, who was able to interpret Mr. Dubois's eye movements. He meticulously transcribed messages so Liz and her father could communicate during the weekly call.

"I'm glad," Jake said. "Well, I better go in."

"I'll wait with you."

"You might be missed in reception," Jake told her.

"It's been dead quiet all day," Liz said.

"You never know when you might be needed."

"I guess you're right. I'll see you later? We can celebrate."

"Sure," Jake said, feeling a stab of disappointment. He'd enjoyed having a couple of hours to himself the previous evening.

Jake watched Liz walk back to the elevator. She hit the button for the lobby and blew Jake a kiss while she waited.

Liz worked behind the reception desk on the ground floor. Jake had been seeing her for a year and had wanted to end things for almost that long. However, the situation with her father made Jake reluctant to break things off. She was a good daughter, saving every cent she made to pay his medical expenses. From the way Liz talked, Jake understood that Mr. Dubois was extremely close to the end of his life.

Once Liz was gone, Jake stepped into the conference room. The empty room lay in darkness. Through the floor-to-ceiling window, Jake saw the lights of Dublin city. They were reflected in the table that ran the length of the room.

He winced at the stale air.

The whole building was stuffy, but this room was especially bad. Sterile, like something Nasa would make if they were trying to simulate the moon. He just couldn't seem to breathe.

Jake flicked on the light. While the fluorescent bulbs flickered to life, he made his way to the other end of the room and opened a window. It only budged a centimetre, to ensure that no one could jump to their death. Grennan and Brennan might have lost some employees over the years otherwise.

Jake smiled at the thought, but it wasn't funny. He'd felt like doing that himself a few times.

The basin of the Grand Canal was below him, a short distance from where the canal met the river. Its water looked calm. The area was quiet today, even the office towers housing the big tech companies. Understandable, the second day after Christmas.

Loosening his tie, Jake leaned forward so his face was near the open window. He tried to suck the freezing air deep into his lungs, but his breathing remained shallow. These last months, he'd felt like he might drop dead any second. His heart was constantly pounding like a rabbit's, his lungs struggling to supply him with oxygen.

Jake's life was enviable. A job at a prestigious law firm. A comfortable apartment. An attentive girlfriend. But somehow this wasn't how he expected life to be.

He walked over to the head of the table and sat in Arthur Grennan's seat. The only comfortable chair in the room, padded with red leather and soft filling.

Jake ran a finger over the polished mahogany tabletop. He couldn't wait to be sitting in this chair for real.

In school, he'd told his guidance counsellor he wanted to work outdoors, doing something on the land. Be a farmer, a park ranger. Stupid idea, but that was where he was happiest. Hiking in the hills, camping by the sea. He kept a Swiss Army knife in the drawer of his desk, as a reminder.

A dark figure in the doorway startled Jake out of his day dream. It was his colleague, Charlotte Flynn.

She said, "Arthur wouldn't like to find you in his chair."

Jake shrugged. "Just seeing how it feels."

Charlotte looked like she'd stepped out of a magazine cover. Her long, brown hair hung in glossy curls on the shoulders of her tailored suit. She wore a crisp navy blouse underneath and a necklace worth more than Jake's apartment.

A stunner, no doubt about it. He'd been attracted to Charlotte since she joined the firm in March. Jake had been dating Liz then. Already trying to get out of it, but it was around then that her father began to really deteriorate.

Charlotte might also have been the best-connected person Jake knew. Her mother was the Chief Justice of Ireland, her father a prominent senator.

No wonder then, that Charlotte walked into the room like she owned the place. She lowered herself into the seat at Jake's side and crossed her legs.

"Better close the window," Charlotte said.

"I need fresh air."

"Arthur gets a chill easily."

"I don't care," Jake snapped.

Charlotte smiled. "You're going to be disappointed today."

"I don't think so."

"Want to bet on it?"

"Sure," Jake said. "How does ten euro sound?"

"Fine for schoolboys. How about ten thousand?"

It took a moment for Jake to realise she wasn't joking. He sat up straighter in his chair. "For real? Ten grand?"

Charlotte cocked an eyebrow. She was for real alright. Jake had about three hundred euro in his bank account. Not that he didn't earn a generous salary, but he couldn't seem to hold onto it. Anyway, it didn't matter whether he had the money. He was certain he'd win the bet. Charlotte was an excellent solicitor, smart and diligent, but she was a newcomer. Jake had been at the firm for a decade, and the promotion was his.

"Fine," Jake said at last.

Charlotte held out a pale hand. Jake reached across the table, took it in his. Her skin was dry, her grip firm.

"Congratulations," Charlotte said. "You just lost ten thousand euro."

Bravado. That was all it was. Charlotte was overconfident.

Jake got to his feet and pushed Grennan's chair in. He walked around to the other side of the table from Charlotte and took a seat as their colleagues began to arrive. Jake greeted people as they entered the room. Charlotte ignored everyone and played with her phone.

The murmuring built as more people arrived. At last, Arthur Grennan walked into the room. The door slammed shut behind him and everyone stopped talking. Grennan was sixty-two years old, thin and slightly stooped, with wisps of white hair doing nothing to hide his scalp. But he showed no sign of stepping down and he still had enough energy to stuff himself into a three-piece suit every day.

Grennan walked up to the top of the table, stopped and looked around, his face puckered up like he'd just bitten into a lemon.

"Christ, there's a draft in here."

"Let me get that," Jake said.

Forcing a smile, he hurried over to the window and closed it. As he sat back down, he sensed Charlotte's eyes on him. He avoided her mocking gaze.

"Now," Grennan said, as he reached the top of the table. "Let us get straight to the point. We are here to welcome the newest partner to this firm."

"Here, here!" someone said.

Jake took a deep breath.

He prepared to stand up.

Arthur Grennan said, "Please join me in congratulating Charlotte Flynn."

CHAPTER TWO

Liz Dubois hadn't been able to resist coming back up to the fifth floor. There was nothing happening downstairs. No reason for her to waste her time in reception. Everyone else was gathered in the conference room.

She lurked in the corridor until everyone was inside, then pressed her ear against the door. She could hardly wait to hear Jake being made a partner. They could celebrate all night. Maybe Jake would stay at her place. She'd missed him the previous evening, but Wednesday nights belonged to her father, and there was nothing she could do about that.

Arthur Grennan began speaking.

Liz held her breath and pressed the side of her head tight against the door.

She gaped in shock when he said Charlotte's name.

How had this happened? Liz couldn't believe Charlotte had stolen the promotion from Jake. It must have been because of her clout. With wealthy, influential parents like hers, Charlotte had never needed to work hard at anything.

It wasn't fair.

Liz strode away from the door, a cold rage sweeping over her as she got into the elevator. She hit the button for the third floor, where the mergers and acquisitions solicitors were based. She wanted to teach Charlotte a lesson.

On the third floor, Liz made her way past the deserted desks to Charlotte's office. It was a sterile room, containing no sign of life. A steel desk, a swivel chair, some shelves and a filing cabinet. No plants. No photos of loved ones. Charlotte had fancy degrees on the wall, and awards lining her shelves.

Liz stood in front of Charlotte's desk.

The computer was on and Liz felt so furious, she thought she might put her fist through the monitor.

Then she caught sight of Charlotte's coat hanging on the rack. Long, belted and black. The label said it was Givenchy. It must have cost Charlotte a fortune. Thousands of euro. It would be a shame if something happened to it.

Liz looked around on the desk for a pair of scissors but couldn't find any. She walked down the hall to Jake's office.

His Swiss Army knife was in its usual place in his top drawer.

CHAPTER THREE

Charlotte pushed back her chair and stood up as her colleagues broke out in applause. They put on a decent show, looking like they were pleased for her – when, really, they all wanted to be where she was.

When Arthur said Charlotte's name, Jake jumped to his feet with a smile. It took a moment for him to realise his name hadn't been called.

"You can sit down," Charlotte said.

Jake did – while everyone laughed.

A little cruel, but Charlotte couldn't afford to show weakness in a room like this.

She shook hands with Arthur. This was a great moment, even if Grennan and Brennan was only the second most prestigious law firm in the country.

"Congratulations, Charlotte."

"Thanks, Arthur."

Up close, his eyes were red and watery, his scalp dotted with liver spots. Two waiters appeared at the back of the room, wheeling in a trolley with ice buckets and champagne flutes. They brought it to the side of the room. Corks shot into the air. Glasses were filled. Everyone got to their feet.

Arthur accepted the first glass of champagne, Charlotte the second.

"I'm driving," she said.

"So is everyone." Arthur smiled. "But a little won't hurt. It's a tradition."

Charlotte had no choice. If these people saw her refuse a glass of champagne, they'd assume she was an alcoholic. Rumours would spread, clients would get edgy. She'd be finished.

"I wouldn't want to stand in the way of tradition," Charlotte said, flashing him her best smile.

Arthur raised his glass to make the toast. "Everyone, please join me in congratulating Charlotte. Not just our new partner, Charlotte will be heading up the Mergers and Acquisitions Department."

With applause ringing in her ears and a smile frozen on her face, Charlotte watched Jake slip out the door.

An uneasy feeling spread across her chest. Surely, he'd known he was never going to be made partner. Charlotte was the logical choice, the most capable solicitor and the one with the best connections. Arthur would have been a fool not to make her partner.

Still, Charlotte took no pleasure in causing Jake distress. She would have already moved on from this firm if he wasn't here.

She took a sip from her glass. The drink fizzed and bubbled in her mouth, the alcohol flavour barely tolerable. Arthur leaned closer to her.

"We're going to be doing some pruning around here," he said in a low voice.

Charlotte nodded slowly. "What did you have in mind?"

"Get rid of the dead wood," Arthur said. "Start with Whelan. He's not pulling his weight."

"You want me to fire Jake?"

"You don't have to do it tonight. But some time before the end of the year."

About as generous as ever.

"Does he really need to go?" Charlotte asked. "You know how bad layoffs can look."

Arthur shrugged. "If you can find a better way to boost the bottom line, it's up to you."

"Understood," Charlotte replied.

As soon as Arthur left to talk to someone else, Charlotte got stuck in a conversation with another senior partner, then a few associates who gathered around her. Charlotte could smell their desperation, their desire for her success to rub off on them.

As soon as she could, Charlotte slipped away to check on Jake. She took the elevator down to the third floor. Jake's office was the same as hers, a grey box with sleek grey furniture, a grey carpet and lots of glass and steel. Jake wasn't at his desk. His jacket was gone.

The Swiss Army knife he was always playing with sat on his desk.

Charlotte made her way to her own office. She saw at once that her new coat hung in tatters.

Someone had cut it up good, stabbing and slicing it mercilessly. Its gold buttons lay all over floor.

Jake.

A feeling of rage swelled within Charlotte's chest. Her mother had taught her never to let a slight go unchecked.

I'll kill that bastard, she thought.

CHAPTER FOUR

Jake stepped out of the elevator on the ground floor. He ignored Liz, who was calling his name, and hurried past the reception desk, out into the night.

The temperature had been hovering around freezing all week, and though there had been no snow on Christmas Day, there was plenty of frost. Jake walked quickly across the pedestrian plaza, next to the canal basin, being cautious not to slip on the ice.

Ten thousand euro, Jake thought. *I've lost ten thousand euro. And didn't get the job I've been working towards for a decade.*

His breathing became more laboured. He pulled out his phone and called Dr. Katherine O'Brien. The counsellor made him call her Kathy. Her clinic would be closed until early January, but Jake couldn't wait that long.

Phone pressed to his ear, he headed for the main road, which ran alongside the pedestrian area. Finally, Kathy picked up.

"I'm sorry to interrupt your holidays," Jake said. "But this is an emergency."

"Slow down. What's happening?"

When Kathy heard the state he was in, she agreed to meet him at a nearby café.

With his hands plunged deep into his pockets, Jake hurried past the tall office blocks. Many big multinationals had extensive office space in the area. Jake wasn't complaining, as they all needed legal advice. But Jake would have preferred to be far away, trekking in the mountains, the smell of pine cones in the air and the soft forest floor under his boots.

These days, he never had time for that. He spent evenings and weekends reading legal documents, in what little time he could steal away from Liz.

As Jake approached the café, he saw Kathy sitting at a stool by the window. He waved and ducked inside.

Aside from a student tapping away on his laptop, they were the only customers.

Jake felt a little better as soon as he caught sight of Kathy. In her mid-forties, she had twinkling amber eyes and an easy smile, her kind face framed by curly red hair. Today she was bundled up in a padded coat. A hat and gloves rested next to a Manilla folder and a steaming cup of tea.

"I planned to treat you," Jake said.

"Never mind. I couldn't wait."

"What are you drinking?"

"Chamomile. You might like to try it sometime."

"I will," Jake said.

But when he went to the counter, he ordered an Americano out of habit.

"This is not what I do," Kathy said, when Jake took the stool next to her. "I'm not an emergency support service."

"I get that," Jake said. "I'm sorry."

"Having said that, I'm willing to make an exception this one time. I've pencilled in twenty minutes and I'm afraid that's all the time I can give you. My kids will be home soon."

"Of course."

"Tell me why you asked to see me."

Kathy listened while Jake spoke about getting passed over for promotion. "It's not just the promotion. It's... I don't know. It's like a cloud hanging over me."

"Like you've told me before?"

"Yeah, but worse. I feel like I'm physically dying now."

"I think being passed over for promotion is a trigger, like some of the other triggers we've discussed."

"It's worse than I've ever felt before. That's what scared me."

He told her how he had feared he'd collapse in the stairwell. Kathy listened and jotted down notes on her pad.

"Remember the progress we've made over the last few weeks," Kathy said. "And remember the tools and techniques that you've successfully employed. The breathing techniques, the meditation, the mindfulness. So whatever the trigger is, we approach the same way, by first observing it and then reviewing our response."

Jake nodded, already feeling better. Amazing how much good a little talking could do. He had no family and he couldn't imagine burdening his friends with this stuff.

When time was up, Jake and Kathy muffled up against the cold and walked outside.

"I'll walk you to your bike," Jake said.

He followed her around the corner, to where a bicycle was chained to a lamppost. The district was eerily quiet.

"That's me," Kathy said.

Jake waited while she removed the lock and got on the saddle. He was glad he'd reached out to her. She had even refused payment for the session.

"Okay," she said, stuffing her notebook in her jacket pocket. "Take care, and make sure to take some time for yourself. This is very important. Self care. I know you hate buzzwords but take some Jake-time."

He smiled. "I will. Thank you."

"Next week, call and make an appointment," she told him.

Kathy cycled out onto the road. As she pedalled, her notebook fell out of her pocket.

"Hey," Jake called.

Kathy glanced over her shoulder. The bike wobbled.

Jake said, "You dropped—"

Then he heard the roar of an engine. A white car tore down the road from the direction of his office.

"Watch out!" Jake shouted.

Kathy raised her arm to shield her eyes from the glare of the headlights, as the car smashed into her.

CHAPTER FIVE

Jake squeezed his eyes shut at the moment of the impact. He heard the dull thump of the car hitting Kathy's body, the chime of her bicycle bell, then the screech of brakes as the car came to a halt.

Kathy was lying motionless on the road when Jake opened his eyes. He stared in horror. The car that had hit her was a white Honda Civic. Jake stepped closer, saw that registration plate indicating that it was seven years old, saw the worn tires and the scratch on the back-right door.

Jake knew this car.

The driver's door opened, and Liz stepped out.

"Oh my god," she gasped.

"Liz?"

Jake's voice was raw. His head felt like it had just finished a spin-and-drain cycle in a washing machine.

He sprinted to the place where Kathy lay motionless. Liz was right behind him. She hunkered down and checked Kathy's pulse. Liz's face was grim when she met Jake's eyes.

"She's dead."

"No." Jake pulled out his phone.

Liz said, "What are you doing?"

"Calling an ambulance. What do you think?"

"No," she said. "We can't help her. She's dead, Jake. Dead. I'm sorry. But no one's going to resuscitate her. Her spine's broken."

Jake supposed he was in shock, as he couldn't seem to think straight. "What are you even doing here?"

"I followed you, of course. You ran off without waiting for me."

"We need to call this in."

"We can't," Liz said. "We'll be in trouble."

"You mean you'll be in trouble."

Liz gave him a hard look. "You distracted me. I saw you at the side of the road, waving your arms in the air." Liz gripped Jake's wrist. "I'm sorry. I'm not blaming you. But the woman's dead. We can't help her. It doesn't make any difference if we tell anyone. All that will happen is we'll get arrested. I can't afford that."

Jake rubbed his eyes, wishing this was just a bad dream. He said, "What do you mean?"

"My dad, Jake. You know his situation. He's able to have an aide looking after him because of my salary. The aide is the only one who can read his eye movements, the only one in the hospital who speaks French. If I'm not sending money, then my dad—"

Jake let out an animal howl of frustration.

He said, "We can't just leave Kathy like this."

Liz touched him on the arm. "I'm sorry. But we have to."

"I'll call it in. Anonymously."

"They'll trace your phone."

"Then drive me to a fucking payphone, Liz."

"Alright, alright," she said. "Don't shout at me."

Jake staggered to front passenger seat of the Honda Civic. Liz got behind the wheel and reversed to the junction behind them.

"Hurry," he said. "Find a phone."

"There are hardly any public phones in Dublin anymore."

"There's one down the road, I think."

"They might still be able to identify you," she said. "What if there's CCTV covering the phone?"

"I don't care. I'm not leaving Kathy there."

"Who is she? What were you doing with her?"

"She's my therapist." Jake's voice caught. "Or she was."

"What?"

Liz turned in surprise.

"God, Liz. Keep your eyes on the road."

"You just never told me you were seeing a therapist. How long were you seeing her? What was it for?"

"It doesn't matter," Jake snapped. He spotted a payphone. "There."

He jumped out of the car before it even stopped moving. He rang for an ambulance, and when the dispatcher started asking questions, he hung up.

Once he was back in the passenger seat, Liz sped away from the area. Jake didn't know where to go, what to do. Part of him wanted to go back to the place where Kathy's body lay, so he could stay with her until an ambulance arrived. He couldn't believe she was dead.

If she hadn't tried to help him, she'd be fine. She'd be with her kids, enjoying the holidays.

"It was a terrible accident," Liz said. "We can't tell anyone about this."

Jake didn't reply.

He hated her for following him. And he hated her for making him leave the scene of the accident. The anger stewed inside him as Liz drove aimlessly around.

Perhaps she was right. What was the point of hanging around when it made no difference to Kathy? He didn't want to see Liz go to jail.

Emerging from a daze, Jake realised they were approaching his apartment. A big old Georgian house on the edge of the city centre, where Jake rented a small apartment.

Liz parked on the street.

In silence, Jake trudged up to his apartment, Liz following close behind.

He opened the door and let her in first. She sat on the couch, curling her feet under her. Jake joined her. For a while, neither of them spoke. The radio in the kitchen was on. Jake sometimes left it on all day as it made the apartment feel less empty when he arrived home with his microwave dinner-for-one.

"Are you okay?" Liz said.

Jake sighed. Said nothing.

The news came on and Jake heard the words "hit and run".

"Did you hear that?" Jake asked. Reporters had already caught wind of the accident. It must have been a slow news day.

"What?"

"Shush." He strained to hear the reporter's words.

"... the woman has been taken to St. Vincent's Hospital and is understood to be in a critical condition. And now for the weather..."

"Oh my god," Jake said.

Kathy was alive.

CHAPTER SIX

When Charlotte saw her ruined coat, she flew into her worst rage for quite a while. She took hold of her swivel chair and slammed it against her desk. Her computer monitor wobbled and her Lawyer of the Year trophy fell to the floor.

Charlotte had planned to do some work, but she was furious at Jake, and she decided she wasn't going to let it go. She rolled up her coat and walked out the door, carrying it under her arm. She took the stairs down to the underground car park. Her silver Jaguar XJ gleamed under a ceiling light.

She threw her coat on the backseat and took a moment to collect herself.

The car smelled faintly of the perfume she'd found at an exclusive boutique in Tuscany over the summer. She'd only been able to get away for a weekend and she'd had to work during the trip. Still, it wasn't so bad. That was simply the kind of sacrifice which ambitious people made.

Charlotte started the engine and drove up the ramp to the street. The new Jaguar purred. It was her first real car, the first one that indicated her status as a woman on her way to the top.

She turned the car in the direction Jake usually walked home. The car was cold from Grennan and Brennan's car park, which was arctic even in summer, and which was now frankly intolerable. Charlotte turned up the heater as she drove through the quiet streets.

The champagne made her light-headed. She hoped she wasn't pulled over and breathalysed. It was possible that she was over the legal limit.

Ahead, she saw a white Honda take a corner like a crazy person. Charlotte eased the Jag to a halt at the junction and watched the car shoot down the road to her right. Twenty, thirty feet away, she caught sight of Jake, talking to a woman on a bike.

The woman on the bike pushed off from the footpath. Charlotte held her breath and watched as the car ploughed straight into her, and screeched to a halt.

Liz got out of the car. She and Jake ran over to the woman. They seemed to argue. After a minute, they both got in Liz's car. It began reversing, moving in Charlotte's direction.

Charlotte put the Jag into reverse too. She eased it into a parking space at the side of the road, then killed the engine.

Liz's Honda stopped once it reached the crossroads. She changed direction and drove straight ahead, through a red light.

Unbelievable, Charlotte thought.

She watched as Liz's car stopped down the road. Jake got out, ran to the footpath. Was that a payphone he was using? They weren't sticking around, but they wanted to report the accident anonymously, Charlotte figured. As soon as Jake got back in the car, it sped away.

Charlotte started the Jag again, drove to where the woman lay on the road, and parked twenty feet away. She got out and made a quick assessment of the victim. A woman in her forties. Head trauma, possible trauma to the lower limbs. The woman was unconscious but still breathing.

"Hold on," Charlotte said. "Help is coming."

At least, she thought it was. She took out her phone and was about to call and make sure an ambulance was on its way when she heard a siren.

At least Jake had the decency to ring it in. But what was going on? Who was the woman? Charlotte noticed a notebook on the tarmac. Grabbing it, she looked at the first page.

Case notes: Jake Whelan.

She flicked through it with interest, decided she'd read it later.

The siren was close. Charlotte wondered whether to wait and tell the paramedics that Liz was responsible, that she and Jake had fled the scene. It would be a fitting punishment, but Charlotte was reluctant to stay when she had alcohol on her breath. And anyway, she had a better idea.

With the notebook in her hand, she hurried back to the Jag. She had only closed her door when the ambulance arrived, screeching to a halt next to the cyclist. Charlotte slowly eased away from the scene.

CHAPTER SEVEN

Jake's apartment was a tight one-bed, with a combined sitting room and kitchen. A tiny bathroom completed the setup. The paint was flaking off the walls in a couple of places near the windows.

Jake thought he'd be doing better by his early thirties. When he was studying law, he'd fantasised about million-euro yachts and three-month cruises on the Riviera – but here he was.

A job he hated, a girlfriend he wanted to dump, and an apartment barely big enough to house his stamp collection. Crazy high rent that devoured most of his income, retail therapy that pissed away the rest. No pension, no family, no time to catch up with friends.

And now this.

Jake walked to the kitchen. He turned the radio off and looked at Liz.

"You said Kathy was dead."

"I'm sure she was. I couldn't find a pulse." Liz shrugged. "I'm not sure. Maybe it was just weak."

"Liz." He shook his head.

"I'm sorry," she said. "I made a mistake. I was under a lot of pressure. But it's good, right?"

"We didn't have to flee the scene. We look like criminals."

Liz got to her feet and followed Jake to the kitchen area. She wrapped her arms around him. "You protected me. Thank you."

Jake said, "I should go to the hospital."

"Are you crazy? They'll think you're responsible."

"I am."

"We both are. But we'll be okay. We have to stay calm."

"I wonder if she'll wake up and remember I was there when it happened."

Liz said, "Did anyone know she was meeting you?"

"I don't think so."

"So let's see what happens. We don't know if she'll recover or not. Even if she's fine, she might not remember the crash."

"What if she does?"

"We'll deal with it." Liz gave him a shaky smile. "Right? We can handle anything together."

Jake felt a surge of guilt that he had thought of dumping her. He hugged Liz back. Together, they returned to the couch, which sat facing the microwave. Handy for when you wanted a snack, but otherwise not ideal.

"How long were you seeing this woman?"

"About a month."

"What for?"

"I just – I needed someone to talk to."

Liz's face fell. "You have me."

"Sure, but—"

"You think it's okay to cheat on me?"

Jake was startled by the venom in Liz's voice. Her face turned pink, her expression hardened.

"What do you mean?" Jake said. He forced a shaky laugh. "Kathy was my counsellor, my therapist. We talked. She was trying to help me."

"So that's fine, is it?"

"Why not? What do you mean?"

Liz sat on the couch as straight as a soldier. Her unblinking eyes stared into Jake's. A second ago, there had been warmth in those eyes. The sudden coldness unnerved him.

"I'm your girlfriend," Liz said. "You should talk to me."

"I do."

"But you needed more?"

He shook his head. "I don't know what you mean."

"Never mind."

Suddenly Liz was walking to the door.

Jake watched her. "Wait, where are you going?"

"I should wash the car. There might be blood on it. Your girlfriend's blood."

"She's my therapist!"

Liz stepped outside and slammed the door behind her. Jake heard her footfalls as she descended the stairs, her feet hitting each step as if it had personally insulted her. Then, the sound of the building's front door slamming.

What was that about?

Jake shook his aching head.

He really did want to go to the hospital, but he supposed Kathy would be in the operating room. Anyway, what right did he have to visit her? She'd taken time out of her holidays because he asked her, and this was her reward.

Jake walked over to the window and looked outside. The street outside was busier than the office district. People walked by, still in a festive mood. A mother and father swung a young girl between them, the child squealing with delight.

Jake thought of Kathy's husband, the kids she had mentioned. Did they know that she was in hospital? Should Jake contact them?

As he was thinking this, his phone buzzed with a text message.

Liz, for sure.

But it wasn't. The message was from Charlotte.

I want to see you in my office.

Fuck, Jake thought. She had been a partner two hours, and already she was trying to boss him around.

He tapped out a reply.

Sure. How about tomorrow after lunch?

His phone buzzed again with Charlotte's reply.

Now.

CHAPTER EIGHT

At Grennan and Brennan's offices, Jake swiped his card so he could pass through the turnstile next to the reception desk. He nodded to Fergal Long, a security guard who had worked at the company even longer than Jake had. Fergal was a taciturn man in his fifties with salt and pepper hair and a bad limp. He'd been a detective until an injury forced him into early retirement. His mind remained as sharp as ever though.

"Back again?" Fergal said.

"I was told to come in."

"We go where we're told, like the fellow said."

Fergal arrived at the office at six every evening. He watched the building until eight the following morning, maintaining himself on a diet of chocolate bars, soft drinks and cat videos, keeping his brain sharp by reading ancient Greek philosophy. He liked to hit young solicitors with brainteasers and words of wisdom.

Jake took the bait. "Who's the fellow that said that? Marcus Aurelius? Aristotle? Socrates?"

Fergal shrugged. "That one? I forget. Maybe that was me?"

Jake forced a smile and kept moving. Sometimes Fergal goofed around but Jake felt nervous being in the presence of a former detective. He felt like guilt was written on his own face for Fergal to read. In the elevator, Jake checked his watch. Only seven thirty, but it felt like midnight.

He stepped out of the elevator on the third floor. Most of his colleagues had gone home and large swathes of the office lay in darkness. What with Christmas, and the partnership announcement, everyone not hurrying home to their families had probably gone to the pub for some festive drinks. Charlotte's brightly lit office stood out.

Jake rapped his knuckles on the door and stepped inside. Charlotte was standing next to her bookshelf, leafing through a journal.

"You wanted to see me?"

Charlotte looked at him.

"Bring me the Kilvian Brewery files. I'm going to handle that from now on."

Jake's mouth fell open. Kilvian Brewery was a great client. He'd got the work through a friend of a friend and had been counting his blessings ever since. The company was riding the craft beer wave.

"What?" was all he could think to say. "Why?"

Charlotte smiled. "I'd like to give them my particular attention."

Jake would be in trouble without that work. Grennan and Brennan expected their employees to bring in cash, lots of it and often.

"You're working fast," Jake said.

"No point wasting time. Go get them."

He retrieved the paper files from his desk and brought them back. He wondered if this was symbolic. The digital file was already on the server for Charlotte to access. Maybe she wanted to humiliate him by making him hand over his paper copies. Well, if that was her intention, it was working. He felt undermined. He'd been just about to send the brewery an invoice, but he supposed Charlotte would take care of that now. He set the files down on her desk.

"Was there anything else?" he asked.

"Draft an e-mail to them for my approval, telling them I'll be their point of contact from now on."

"Draft an e-mail for your approval?" Jake snorted. "Like I'm your secretary?"

Charlotte walked across the room, stopping just in front of Jake. He caught the scent of her perfume.

She said, "How are the panic attacks?"

"What?"

"Better? Worse? Are you still crying as you walk to work in the mornings? Dreaming of throwing yourself in the canal but too chickenshit to do it?"

Jake flushed. "How did – where did you get that idea?"

"I have my sources," Charlotte said.

Jake had told no one at work about the panic attacks. Not even Liz. The only person on earth he'd told was Kathy.

Jake said, "I have no idea what you're getting at, but—"

"What did you buy Liz for Christmas?"

"Charlotte—"

"You should have given her some driving lessons."

Jake's heart hammered in his chest. "I have no idea—"

Charlotte said, "Don't play innocent. I know what you and your girlfriend did. Arthur wouldn't look kindly on employees carrying out hit-and-runs. It's considered bad form in the legal profession. Your careers would be over, of course, not that Liz was every going to amount to much. If the woman dies, Liz is looking at a charge of involuntary manslaughter. You'll go down for secondary participation."

Charlotte went over to her desk and picked up a notebook.

"Interesting reading. I had no idea you were so close to cracking."

After a moment, Jake realised what Charlotte held in her hands. Kathy's notes. The ones she'd dropped on the street before the accident. Charlotte must have been there, and seen what happened, must have come along afterwards and picked the notebook up.

Jake's mouth went dry.

Charlotte *knew*.

His life hung in her hands. Public shame, censure, long term unemployment, years in jail.

In a low voice he said, "Did you report it?"

"Not yet. But I can change that anytime. People are looking for you and Liz."

Jake made a grab for the notebook, but Charlotte pulled it out of his reach.

"Don't be stupid," she said with a laugh. "I have photos of these notes stored online."

"Are you joking me?"

"No, I'm not. It always pays to be careful. That's a lesson Liz could have done with."

Jake imagined Liz being taken away in cuffs. Her father, left alone, with no one to speak to, and no aide to speak through. It would kill him.

"Please don't report this," Jake said. "It was an accident."

"Why did you run then?"

"We thought she was dead. It was a mistake."

"Yes," Charlotte said, "It was a mistake, alright."

CHAPTER NINE

Liz parked under a lamppost in front of her building. The estate consisted of three blocks, each of them red brick, seven storeys tall, solid and neat. They'd been built in the seventies and occupied by countless young professionals since then, in the lonely years before starting a family. Liz knew that loneliness too well.

She had driven around the city for a long time, feeling uneasy. Feeling hurt, if she was honest. With the window open, she smoked cigarette after cigarette, ignoring the freezing air's bite, focusing instead on the nicotine rush. She'd more or less given up smoking, as Jake didn't like her tobacco breath.

Jake.

She couldn't understand him. He saw nothing wrong with opening up to some glorified agony aunt, while keeping his feelings a secret from her, his life partner. She wished he'd call. She had been sure he'd follow her when she stormed out of his apartment, but he hadn't. The important thing was to be together, especially at a time like this. But her phone had remained silent.

Liz stared at the closest apartment block, where she lived on the ground floor. This place was not ideal, but she wasn't able to afford luxury on a receptionist's salary – even a receptionist at a fancy law firm.

Soon things would change, though.

Liz and Jake would get married. She'd start studying. She'd become a lawyer too. She wasn't old, only thirty-four. There was time to start again.

Maybe have a couple of children.

Jake would make partner next year, no doubt about it, and their combined salaries would let them buy a house somewhere nice. They might not be able to afford Dublin, but one of the commuter towns in Kildare was probably within reach. She wouldn't mind commuting to work every day, only an hour or so each way, and she'd have her husband sitting next to her the whole way.

Liz had a smile on her face when she stepped out of the car.

She hit the key fob as a voice boomed out of the darkness.

"What's up?"

A figure was moving towards her across the lot. A tall man with powerful shoulders. He stepped into the light, eyes gleaming like a wolf's.

Liz recognised Colin McMahon. He lived on the floor above her and worked as a barista at Starbucks. He'd been flirting with her ever since she moved into the building. Asking her out, asking how she was, every time their paths crossed in the car park or the laundry room. She'd done nothing to encourage him, but even her thick-framed glasses hadn't put him off.

"Jesus, Colin, you scared the shit out of me."

He laughed. "Why are you so nervous?"

Liz shrugged. "Everywhere is so quiet. And then…"

"Boom! Yeah, I get it. Were you working today?"

"Yeah. You too?"

"Sure, have to keep the customers caffeinated."

Colin was a big, strong guy with a huge head and tiny impish eyes buried under V-shaped brows. She always thought he looked like he was halfway through transforming into a werewolf.

"Right." Liz swung her handbag over her shoulder. "I better be going."

"What happened to your car?"

Liz's muscles tensed.

"What do you mean?"

Colin walked around the front.

"The scratch there? And the bump? The bonnet's a little dented. Not to mention… that looks like blood."

Liz's mouth dropped open. "What? Where?"

Colin pointed. "There and there and there."

Fuck. He was right. Liz saw red smears of blood.

"Oh, that. I hit a deer."

"A deer?" Colin's eyes widened. "Where? Got a better chance of winning the lottery than hitting a deer in Dublin."

"Lucky me, I guess."

Liz swallowed. She hadn't expected a cross-examination, but it had been stupid to park under the light.

"I'm going inside," she said. "It's cold."

Colin reached out, gripped her arm above the elbow and held it tight.

He said, "Well, it's funny, but I was listening to the news as I drove home. I heard about an accident. A hit-and-run."

"Oh?"

"You didn't hear? I guess you were too busy driving through deer country. Where is that, by the way? Deer country?"

"Um…"

Colin shook his head like it didn't matter.

"Funny. I usually remember where I was ten minutes ago. But maybe I'm strange. Anyhow, the news—"

"Let go of me."

Colin looked at his hand as if he'd forgotten he was holding her. He let go, loosening each finger theatrically.

She set off walking away from him.

"That news show," Colin called after her. "The one I heard, they said someone knocked a lady down. In the south inner city. That's where you work, isn't it?"

Liz said, "So what?"

"So nothing. I just thought you might want to drink a beer with me. We could have a chat. Unwind after a long day."

"I don't think so. I have things to do."

She kept walking.

"I just hope you don't get in any trouble," Colin said.

Liz stopped, turned around. Colin had an infuriatingly smug look on his face.

"Come again?" Liz said.

"If someone saw all that blood on your car, they might get the wrong idea. Think you had something to do with that hit-and-run that happened near your office."

Did he really suspect her? It was such rotten luck that he had seen the car. Liz couldn't risk ending up in jail, having Jake end up in jail. She couldn't let anything keep them apart. Maybe she needed to play Colin's game.

Liz said, "That's the worst chat-up line I've ever heard."

"Sorry. I'm not very smooth. My brain shoots around from topic to topic. I just thought we could chill out and have a beer. Relax after a long day, right?"

"I guess I am thirsty. One beer?"

"Or wine if you like. I have wine too."

"At your place?"

"Sure. I'm not driving anywhere."

Liz said, "Alright. A drink might help me unwind."

Colin caught up with her and took her hand in his. So they were going to pretend he wasn't blackmailing her. Liz resisted the urge to pull away. She was in trouble. That was for sure. But she had no idea know how much.

CHAPTER TEN

Colin's apartment was on the first floor, almost directly above Liz's. She wondered what his place was like. Maybe the walls were painted black, a cross hung upside-down on the wall and the sink was piled high with festering dishes. She braced herself as he unlocked his door.

As she stepped inside, she realised it wasn't so bad. The apartment was bare, with pale blue walls and a few pieces of furniture from Ikea.

"Let me give you the tour," Colin said as he closed the door. He paused a second and said, "Well, I hope you enjoyed the tour."

The apartment's layout was similar to that of her own place. The front door led into a small sitting room. A corridor led to a tiny bedroom, a kitchen and a bathroom.

"You live alone?"

"Sure," Colin said. "Is it like your place?"

"A bit."

"I'd like to see that for myself sometime."

Liz coughed so she wouldn't have to answer. Colin was never getting inside her apartment. That was for sure.

The main feature in the sitting room was a huge TV. Underneath it lay a PlayStation and two controllers. A square table with a laptop and speakers sat in the corner.

Colin hung his jacket on the back of a chair and powered up the laptop.

The car, Liz thought.

She had to get back to it before someone else noticed the signs of an accident.

"Red or white? I have a little of both left over from Christmas."

It took Liz a moment to realise he was talking about wine. "Actually, I'd like a beer."

Colin nodded with approval. "A beer-drinking chick? Alright, I like it."

He went into the kitchen. Liz heard the sound of a fridge opening.

"The building's so quiet," Liz said. Colin came back and handed her a bottle. No glass. Cap still on.

"Good, isn't it?"

"I think it's kind of creepy."

Colin used a bottle opener on his keyring to pop his own bottle's cap, then sank down on one side of the couch. Perhaps out of habit, he glanced at the TV.

"Sit down," he said.

Liz did, leaving a space between them, but Colin scooted nearer to her. She accepted the bottle opener from him. After popping the cap, she looked around for somewhere to put it.

"Just throw it on the floor," Colin said.

"Are you nuts? I can't do that."

"I don't own the place."

"Doesn't matter."

Colin took a swig of beer. "Do you have OCD?"

Liz went to the kitchen, where she found the bin. She also found a knife block on the kitchen counter. Five knife handles stuck out of the wood. Solid steel, judging by the look of them.

Liz reached out for the nearest knife. Her fingers had just touched the cold handle when heavy metal music filled the air at a deafening volume. A raging wall of distorted guitars, pounding bass and thundering drums.

Liz took a breath to steady herself.

She threw the bottle cap into the bin and returned to the sitting room. Colin was leaning over his laptop. He glanced at her over his shoulder.

"Alright?"

He turned the speaker up louder.

Colin couldn't have been less like Jake. Jake, with his Beethoven and his Handel and, when he really went wild, jazz. Liz felt a headache coming on.

"Could you turn it down a little?"

"What?"

She gestured downwards with her hand.

"What?" Colin said, with a hand to his ear.

Liz leaned in. "I said, could you—"

Colin turned down the music. Then he grabbed her. Got in her face. His stubble scratched her chin as he found her mouth and pressed his tongue inside.

She tried to pull away, but he held her in place. With an urgency that startled her, Colin pressed his body against her.

His disgusting tongue probed her mouth, his saliva mingling with her own. He towered over her, huge and powerful.

Liz gagged.

Colin only stopped kissing her when Liz bit his tongue hard enough to draw blood.

She followed that up by driving her knee into his crotch.

He doubled over and his face turned purple.

"Fucking bitch," he wheezed.

Tiny droplets of blood flew out of his mouth when he spoke.

Liz wondered if she had time to get to the knives, or if he'd kill her before she reached the kitchen.

CHAPTER ELEVEN

Jake's throat went dry as he gazed at Charlotte, who had the power to ruin Liz's life and his too, if he wasn't careful.

"So let me get this straight," Jake said. "You're not going to tell anyone what happened, but you're going to hold this over me forever? That's what you're telling me?"

Charlotte smiled. "I'm simply telling you where you stand."

"Which is nowhere."

"I thought you'd understand," Charlotte said. "I expect that ten thousand euro to be in my bank account by the end of the week."

Jake swallowed.

"I don't have it," he said. He had no way to get it either, unless the bank was willing to give him a loan.

Charlotte sat down behind her desk and turned her attention to her computer. She said, "You better figure out how to get it. By the way, did you know you're being paid significantly less than other associates?"

"How do you know that? Is that true?"

"It's true."

"Why?" He felt a surge of outrage.

"I'll let you think about it for yourself. Now go home."

Like a beaten dog, Jake dragged himself out of her office and headed for the bank of elevators. The whole evening felt a nightmare. Being passed over for promotion, the car crash, and now Charlotte blackmailing Jake into doing whatever she wanted… forever.

She could boss him around, and there would be nothing he could do. Not if he and Liz wanted to stay out of jail.

Jake's life had gone into free-fall.

What was he going to do?

His stomach roiled.

Maybe what she'd said about backing up Kathy's notebook online was a bluff. Maybe not. Charlotte was meticulous. Jake wouldn't have dreamt of hurting her anyway. He didn't want his therapist's case notes to be revealed, but he would never have thought of hurting Charlotte to stop that happening. The last time Jake had been in a physical fight, he'd been about five years old. He didn't possess that killer instinct some of his colleagues seemed to have. He just wanted to have a quiet life.

Jake was still thinking when he walked straight into Arthur Grennan.

The managing partner appeared out of nowhere in the corridor. Jake ploughed into him, knocking the old man on his backside.

Grennan let out a gasp of pain as he crumpled on the floor.

"Jesus, Arthur, I'm sorry."

"You *idiot*."

Jake flinched at the rebuke, but he helped Grennan to his feet.

"Are you okay? I'm so sorry."

"Look where you're going."

"I didn't know anyone else was here."

"What are you doing here?"

"I was just… I was getting a file for Charlotte."

Grennan snorted. Jake could almost read his mind. *Getting files is all you're good for.*

Jake said nothing as the old man hobbled past him, down the corridor.

"Shit," Jake whispered.

He pressed the button for the elevator and stepped inside.

Going down.

CHAPTER TWELVE

Liz sprinted down Colin's hallway, through the open doorway into the kitchen. The knife block was on the counter. She threw herself at it as Colin staggered after her. She could feel his breath on the back of her neck, could smell the beer on his breath. His hand slapped against the doorjamb behind her as he struggled for purchase.

"Come back here," he snarled.

Liz's hands were clumsy, fumbling with one knife handle and then another. She glanced over her shoulder and saw Colin advancing on her, breathing hard. An expression of blind rage spread over his face. He seemed to have grown two feet taller since he got mad. She wasn't going to be able to sweet-talk her way out of this one.

She finally got a grip on the biggest knife in the block at the same time that Colin grabbed her shoulder, pulling her around.

As she turned, she lashed out, stabbing at Colin.

He grunted when she nicked his chin.

Liz lunged forward again, knife first. Colin grabbed the blade with his fingers, and Liz forced the sharp edge down, cutting deeper into his flesh, drawing a howl of agony from Colin's mouth. She pulled the blade away, then lashed out again.

It sliced through the air, hitting nothing, but Colin jerked backwards to avoid the blade. His head smashed hard into the doorframe.

Thank god, Liz thought.

A moment of surprise, of disorientation.

She lost no time throwing herself at him. But she wasn't fast enough. Colin saw her coming and thrust a massive fist at her. It hit her arm, just above the wrist. The knife fell from her fingers, clattering on the kitchen tiles. Liz fell on her backside.

At once, Colin was on top of her, pinning her down.

"Let me up."

"You fucking cut me."

"I said, let me up."

He gave her an appraising look.

"I didn't believe you did that hit-and-run. I was only playing. Now I'm not so sure."

"I don't care what you think."

"Now I can believe it. I can believe you—"

"I said I don't care, asshole."

He slapped her across the face with the back of his hand, knocking her glasses onto the floor. The world blurred.

"Shut your bitch mouth."

He unbuckled his belt and pulled it out of the loops in his jeans. Liz watched him, a roaring sound filling her ears.

"You know why I'm going to enjoy this?" Colin undid the button on his jeans and began to zip his fly down. "Because you're going to see that you're no better than I am. Oh, I know, you walk around like you're so great. Not anymore."

He was smiling, confident that he was in charge. He didn't realise Liz had another blade. Not as sharp as the kitchen knife, but sharp enough.

She worked her hand into the pocket of her jacket slowly, and clasped Jake's Swiss Army knife. She waited until Colin shifted his weight, so he could wriggle one leg out of his jeans, and then she pulled out the knife.

Colin saw it. Saw Liz's other hand reach over and pull the blade open.

His eyes widened, but he was off-balance.

Liz stabbed it into Colin's thigh as hard as she could.

He howled like a pig. Liz shoved him off her. She was on her feet in a second, scooping up her glasses and putting them on, looking around for something, anything, to defend herself with.

Colin was already pushing himself up from the tiles.

A meat tenderiser caught Liz's eye. It was a mean-looking hammer with dozens of sharp metal points. Good for pounding dumb meat.

Liz grabbed it off the counter. Turning, she smashed it into the side of Colin's head.

He went down without a sound.

Liz slumped on the floor next to him.

Her breathing was ragged, her ears pulsing with blood, its flow as fast as the heavy metal music had been.

She sat on the floor with her legs crossed, willing her breathing to return to normal. Once its frantic pace had slowed, Liz glanced at the mess around her.

The unconscious man.

The blood.

This is going to be hard to explain, she thought.

Then the doorbell rang.

CHAPTER THIRTEEN

After Jake left, Charlotte decided to stay at the office to get more work done. As a new partner, there was much to do, though of course she had been preparing for this day for years.

When she went to the canteen to grab a coffee, she saw Arthur Grennan.

He was stalking the corridors like a vulture, muttering to himself, his face pink, his lips cracked from the cold air. Charlotte thought it best to stay out of his way.

The canteen was closed, but she slipped behind the counter to make herself a coffee.

As the water boiled, Charlotte thought of the tantalising rumour her father had told her. Soon the government would appoint Arthur as a High Court judge. He'd have to give up his job in the firm in order to accept the position. If that happened, Charlotte was confident she'd be able to take over as managing partner.

She brought her coffee back to her desk. This was the last night she'd sit in this chair. Tomorrow morning a larger office would await, with "CHARLOTTE FLYNN, PARTNER" emblazoned across the door.

As she took a sip of coffee, her phone rang. It was her mother.

"Sorry for disturbing you, Charlotte. Can you talk?"

"Yes, it's fine. I did it. I made partner."

"Of course, you did, Charlotte. We knew you'd be successful."

Charlotte smiled. "I thought so, but you can never be sure."

"And what about that fellow you work with? How disappointed was he?"

Charlotte pictured Jake standing up when her name was called. The pained look on his face as he hurried from the conference room.

"Very disappointed," she said. "But that's nothing to do with me. Jake didn't earn it."

"Don't you still like him? Are you going to ask him out?"

Thump.

Charlotte remembered the sound of Liz's car smashing into the therapist's body. Then she pictured Jake in her office a few minutes earlier. The pathetic look on his face.

She couldn't believe she'd ever thought he might make a desirable partner. The prospect was laughable.

"Things have become complicated," Charlotte said.

"Yes, well, maybe he isn't the right type anyway. Not enough fire in his belly."

"That's true," Charlotte said.

Or maybe he just hasn't learnt to kindle it yet.

"On the other hand," her mother said, "remember Lucy Reynolds. You know how much I love Lucy. She's my best friend, after all, but she was alone all her life because she was so fussy. No one was ever good enough."

"I'm not fussy. But I have standards."

"You sound just like Lucy."

"No, I don't."

"Lucy is so lonely now that she's retired. All she does these days is collect ceramic figurines. It's deranged. You know what I've always loved about your father?"

Charlotte sighed. "Yes."

"It bears repeating. I've always loved him because he has a kind heart. Even if he is a politician. Most people might not even believe he has a heart. But you know how he is. Beneath that hard-as-nails facade, he's a big sweetie."

"I know." Charlotte's tone was sharper than she'd meant. "I know," she said more gently.

"There's a lot you can forgive a good man."

Not mutilating a Givenchy coat, Charlotte thought.

"I need to get back to work," she said, ending the call.

There was a meeting tomorrow she needed to prepare for, and it shouldn't take more than three or four hours. This was why Charlotte was made partner and Jake was not. He was not willing to do the unpleasant things that sometimes had to be done.

CHAPTER FOURTEEN

Jake got on a number 7 bus, headed for St. Vincent's Hospital. Unable to face going home, he hoped he might be able to get some news about Kathy's condition if he went to the hospital.

He took a seat at the back, next to a sullen teenage boy in a puffy black jacket and grey tracksuit bottoms. The boy's hair was skin-tight at the back and sides and sprouting like a vegetable from the top of his head. His phone blared. Music and snatches of video clips. The only other person on the lower deck was an old woman huddled up at a window seat halfway down the bus.

At least the bus was warm. Jake could feel hot air blasting from the vents behind him. He had waited twenty minutes in the freezing cold.

Jake wasn't sure what he'd do if Kathy was not alright. He stared out the window feeling more wretched than ever before.

Beside him, the boy was now talking loudly on the phone. Normally Jake would have done nothing, just tolerated the selfish behaviour, but he was so far outside of his comfort zone right now, the boundary lines were a blur.

"Hey, be quiet," Jake said.

The teenager gave him a look. He said, "Fuck off," then turned away.

Rage boiled up inside Jake's brain.

"No, fuck you," Jake snapped. He grabbed the phone and smashed it against the handrail. There was a crunch of glass on metal as the screen broke. Jake turned and flipped open the window. The boy grabbed him from behind, but Jake ignored him and lobbed the phone out the window.

"No one wants to hear your shit," he said, closing the window.

The boy put his hands to his head and said, "You bollocks."

Jake formed a fist and hit the boy once in the mouth, his knuckles closed tight and his arm straight, the way he'd been taught in karate class when he was a kid.

The boy tumbled onto the floor, probably more surprised than hurt, uttered a muffled threat, then ran to the front of the bus, where he shouted at the driver. But the bus kept going until the next stop. As soon as the door opened, the teenager jumped out.

Jake flashed the boy the finger as he walked past the window. He saw with satisfaction that a few drops of blood coloured his lips.

Jake leaned back in his seat as the bus started moving again. A warm feeling of satisfaction filled him. The old woman had turned in her seat and looked at Jake.

"Sorry about that," he said.

The woman turned away without a word.

The happy feeling stayed with Jake until the bus approached the hospital. He pressed the button and walked to the front of the bus.

"Nice one," the driver said, giving Jake a wink as the door opened.

Jake wondered how often the driver had wanted to give some unruly passenger a punch.

He stepped off the bus, onto a deserted footpath. Various hospital buildings loomed out of the darkness on the other side of the road.

He crossed at the pedestrian lights, which took him to the shopping centre beside the hospital. Then he waited to cross the next road, over to the hospital.

His phone began to ring as he stood there. The screen said, "LIZ CALLING". He put it back in his pocket without answering, as the light turned green for him to cross the road.

He made his way up a stone path to the main hospital building, past a few hardy smokers, and through the electric doors. Light and heat hit him at the same time.

He stepped in front of a passing nurse, a young Indian woman.

"I'm looking for Dr. Katherine O'Brien. She was the victim of a hit-and-run."

The young woman nodded. "Are you family?"

"No. I'm a friend."

She pulled Jake out of the way of a passing stretcher.

"I'm afraid you can't see her now."

"I know it's late. I'm sorry. But I'm a good friend. Can you tell me anything?"

The nurse sighed.

"The patient came out of surgery ten minutes ago, but she has not regained consciousness."

"Is she okay?"

The nurse spoke slowly. "We will have to assess her condition when she wakes up. All we can say for now is that she is stable."

Jake nodded.

"Thank you," he said.

At least Kathy was alive.

So far.

CHAPTER FIFTEEN

Liz slipped her phone in her pocket. She really needed to talk to Jake but he wasn't answering. She stood in the doorway of Colin's kitchen and listened.

The doorbell rang again.

Colin was unconscious, flat on his back on the floor. He hadn't moved since she hit him on the side of the head with the meat-tenderiser.

Was he breathing?

She was afraid to check.

Afraid he'd reach out and grab her.

She crept to the door and peered through the peephole. Two young men were standing in the corridor. Rough-looking men. Each of them was carrying a six-pack of beer. Friends of Colin? He hadn't mentioned anything about having friends over, but that didn't mean much. The thought of getting Liz into his apartment might have swept everything else out of his mind.

One of the men stepped forward and banged on the door.

"Hey Colin? Open up, man."

Liz watched through the glass as the other guy pulled out a phone.

As quietly as she could, she made her way back to the kitchen, just as Colin's phone began to ring. The ring tone was like an old-fashioned telephone.

Brrring, Brrring.

It was coming from somewhere on Colin. She crouched down. The phone had to be in his jeans, which were bundled around his knees. Her fingers shook as she slipped them into the right front pocket.

Nothing there but a ball of snotty tissues, all wet and squishy.

Colin emitted a soft moan. She waited to see if he would move.

The phone continued ringing.

Brrring, Brrring.

Its sound was muffled, but she needed to silence it before the men outside heard. She hoped they would go away. But if Colin had invited them to his place, they'd wonder what had happened to him, why he wasn't answering.

Liz slipped her hand into Colin's other pocket. She found the phone straight away, wedged in next to his wallet. Liz pulled the phone out and rejected the incoming call.

She turned the phone off.

Hopefully Colin's friends would get bored and leave.

"Uuhhh…"

Colin moaned softly.

His arm twitched.

If he called for help, she was done for. They'd burst in and see what she'd done. The three of them would gang-rape Liz and kill her. She had no doubt about it. Colin seemed like that kind of guy, and his friends looked the same.

She opened the kitchen drawers one by one, looking for anything useful. She found a ball of twine in the second drawer. It would have to do. In the same drawer, she found a pair of nail scissors.

Liz needed a gag too.

She opened the cupboard under the sink. A foul-looking dish cloth sat on a soap dish. Liz didn't want to touch the cloth, but she forced herself to pick it up.

She brought everything over to the place on the floor where Colin lay sprawled. He looked awful in the unforgiving glare of the fluorescent light. Waxy, like a corpse laid out for viewing.

She crouched down and tied his ankles together, hoping he was still too out-of-it to notice. Once his legs were secure, she moved onto his hands.

She knew she'd have to be fast, in case he felt her tying him up.

Liz took a breath, then set to work, bringing the two wrists together and wrapping the twine around them.

She'd made only a couple of passes when Colin coughed and pulled his hands apart.

He was waking up.

Outside, his friends banged on the door again.

She pulled Colin's hands together again and held them with one hand while running circles of twine around them with the other.

Colin's eyes fluttered open. He blinked at Liz.

She finished tying a knot just as he realised what she was doing to him.

He opened his mouth wide to scream, to call for help – and Liz shoved the dish cloth into his mouth, muffling his screams.

He still managed to make too much noise though. Liz pushed the cloth in deeper.

"Quiet," she said.

Colin glared at her, his face turning purple.

Liz stood up. Jake's pen knife still stuck out of Colin's thigh. She'd stuck him with it pretty nice. She yanked the knife out. Colin jerked and his muffled screaming became more intense. Liz stepped aside and watched him.

What a waste of energy.

He couldn't go anywhere.

She walked to front door and looked through the peephole. Colin's friends were walking away.

Relieved, Liz slumped on the couch, exhausted after the ordeal. She needed a moment to cool off. Good thing she'd taken Jake's penknife. It had come in handy, not only for slicing up Charlotte's dress but for sticking that piece of shit in the kitchen.

Liz wondered what Jake was doing.

She hoped Charlotte wasn't going to start throwing her weight around now that she was a partner. Liz wasn't about to let anyone keep Jake away from her.

CHAPTER SIXTEEN

Leaving the hospital, Jake couldn't help feeling dispirited. But at least Kathy had not died. He walked through the automatic doors and stepped outside, immediately finding himself swallowed by the dark night.

Jake crossed the road to the supermarket. He walked the aisles aimlessly. The growling of his stomach reminded him he was hungry, yet he couldn't decide what to eat. In the end, he left without buying anything.

He set off walking towards home, gazing blankly at the huge houses he passed. Charlotte would one day live in this kind of neighbourhood. With a Maserati parked behind an electric gate. CCTV cameras and a fancy security system to protect her.

This place wasn't for Jake.

I used to think I was smart.

But he had been wrong. Being passed over for partner again was evidence of that. The hit-and-run was more. Not only was he stupid, but he was a coward.

I've turned into a shitty person, Jake thought.

But when? And how had it happened?

His phone buzzed. Liz was calling.

No hello when he picked up. She said, "I need you, Jake."

"Liz, I feel sick."

"What? Where are you?"

"I went to the hospital."

"What's wrong with you?" Liz sounded almost hysterical.

"I went to check on Kathy but they wouldn't let me see her."

"Are you crazy? Don't go near that woman. Look, I need you to come to my place. We have another problem."

Jake frowned. He couldn't imagine how things might get any worse. He didn't even want to know.

"Okay," he said. "I'm on my way."

As he hung up the phone, his stomach rumbled again. Ignoring it, he changed course, walking towards Liz's place.

It took twenty minutes to get there, walking through the dark streets. When he passed a family, perhaps walking home from the shops or from visiting family, their high spirits just about broke his heart. Two adults and two kids. A perfect little family.

Soon he reached Liz's road. He ducked into the entrance to her estate, saw three large blocks of apartments ahead. Jake realised his fingers were numb. He'd forgotten to wear gloves, a hat or a scarf.

And the jacket he was wearing was too light for this weather.

He set off across the car park towards the building.

"Jake?"

He turned towards the sound. Liz was walking towards him, carrying a bucket in one hand. She looked awful. Haggard and tired, as if she had aged ten years during the day.

He said, "What are you doing?"

"I needed to wash the car."

"Why did you need to…"

Because of the blood, he realised.

Kathy's DNA was on the car, and Liz was cleaning away the evidence of their crime. That must be why she wanted him there. To help her. Or so he would be complicit in this too. They were bound together by this accident.

Liz said, "I'll need to get the dents fixed too, but—"

His stomach heaved at the thought of Kathy's blood splashed across the white paintwork.

Liz said, "Are you okay?"

Jake nodded, though his mouth was flooding with saliva. He hurried over to the strip of grass behind the cars and vomited in the grass.

He stayed bent over, waiting to see if he would be sick again. And he was. Another spurt of vomit shot from his mouth just as Liz reached him and put a hand on his back.

"I'm sorry," Jake said, straightening up. "I have to go."

"What?"

Jake didn't wait for an answer. He turned away and set off walking briskly in the direction he had just come from. He ignored Liz when she called his name.

CHAPTER SEVENTEEN

Liz's throat tightened as she watched Jake hurry across the car park. He couldn't leave her alone. She needed him.

"Jake? Wait."

"I'm sorry," he muttered, without looking back.

She ran after him, catching up with him as he reached the street, grabbing his arm at the elbow.

"Jake."

He shook off her hand without looking.

"Sorry, Liz. I can't do this right now."

He set off down the road. The chill air suddenly felt colder. Only the plastic bucket Liz held in one hand was remotely warm, from the warm water she'd used to wash her car. To wash the blood away.

She understood Jake being emotional. He was a sensitive man. But she was in trouble. She needed him.

She thought of the *Good luck* card she had given him. *To Jake, my partner.*

They were in this together.

She hadn't been given a chance to tell him that Colin knew their secret. She really wanted Jake's help to figure out what to do about that, but it seemed she'd have to handle it on her own.

She walked back the way she had come, passing her car and entering the apartment building. She got the elevator to Colin's floor, and let herself into his apartment.

Colin still lay tied up and gagged on the kitchen floor. When he saw her, he tried to speak. She stepped over him and began to fill up the bucket with more hot water.

"Are you calm?" Liz asked.

Colin glared at her in reply. He was a sorry sight, with his pants around his ankles and blood running down his legs from where she'd stabbed him. A trickle of blood ran down the side of his head from when she had hit him with the meat tenderiser. The floor tiles were smeared with blood. Liz was relieved that the twine at his ankles and wrists had held strong.

Maybe she could talk to him now. They might be able to reason this out, like two sensible adults. Something unfortunate had happened, but that didn't mean they couldn't move past it.

She hunkered down and pulled the dish cloth out of his mouth.

"You fucking stupid bitch. I'm gonna fucking kill you, you—"

"Let's talk about this calmly, okay?"

"You're so fucking dead. I'm gonna rip your stupid head off and shit down your neck."

Colin's face turned an apoplectic shade of purple. A vein bulged at the side of his forehead.

She shoved the cloth back in his mouth.

Liz said, "I give you one chance, and that's what you say to me? You threaten me? Use crude language and insult me? You're the stupid one."

Colin jerked his head from side to side and thrashed around with his body. He grunted loudly. Too loudly.

Liz waited until he'd stopped moving around so much. Then she grabbed his head with one hand and, with the other, she shoved the gag in deeper.

She walked over to the sink, where the bucket was overflowing with water, turned off the tap and lifted the bucket. It was heavy, but she had to carry it.

Panting and fighting for breath, her arms aching, Liz brought the bucket out to the car and emptied the hot water over the bonnet. Then she moved the car to a darker corner of the car park. She'd like to avoid letting people see the dent, if she could.

When she was done, she brought the empty bucket back upstairs to Colin's place.

He didn't move or make a sound this time, even when Liz set the bucket down on the floor next to his face.

"Are you calm?" she asked again. She wondered if it was worth trying to reason with him one more time.

She hunkered down and slapped Colin's face.

He wasn't calm.

He was dead.

CHAPTER EIGHTEEN

The next morning, Jake arrived at the office feeling like a zombie. The two cups of coffee he'd drank as he stood in his kitchen couldn't compensate for the lack of sleep. He'd been awake all night, hoping that Kathy would pull through.

Liz had called him twenty-seven times. He ignored her. Judging by the times of the phone calls, she didn't sleep either.

As he pushed through the gleaming glass doors of Grennan and Brennan, he caught sight of her sitting behind the reception desk. She had bags under her bloodshot eyes, but was smartly dressed and had done full make-up as usual. The lobby was empty. She leaned forward when she saw him.

"We need to talk," Liz hissed.

"Later," Jake said. "I'm going to call the hospital. I was waiting until a reasonable hour. Now should be okay."

"Jake."

"I said, later, Liz."

It seemed like everyone wanted to push Jake around and he was getting sick of it.

Jake saw Charlotte in her office. She was absorbed in something on her computer screen. He hurried past her office to his own.

Once there, he closed the door and slumped in his chair. He picked up the desk phone and phoned St. Vincent's. The call was transferred to a nurses' station.

"I was hoping to find out how Dr. Katherine O'Brien is doing."

A woman with an Indian accent answered. "Are you family?"

"No."

"I can't tell you anything if you are not family."

"I'm her friend. I visited last night."

A pause.

Please, Jake thought.

"The good friend?"

"That's right," he said. "I think you and I talked briefly. What's your name?"

"Shilpa."

"I'm sorry to bother you, Shilpa, but I'm really worried about Dr. O'Brien. I was up all night thinking about her. Can you just tell me if she's got better or worse?"

"She woke up an hour ago," Shilpa whispered.

Jake broken out in a huge grin. "That's fantastic," he said.

"She is not out of the woods yet, but she is doing better."

"Wonderful. Thank you so much. Thank you, Shilpa."

"You're welcome."

It was like a crushing weight had been lifted. Jake had been sure Kathy would die or stay in a coma. It was a massive relief to hear she was improving. Liz would be delighted.

Jake hurried out of his office.

He took the elevator back down to reception.

Two young men in jeans and hoodies were sitting on the couches in front of the reception desk. They looked like college students who'd got lost. One was thin, with straggly long hair and round glasses. The other was pink faced, with brown hair cut so uniformly short that he resembled a kiwi. Jake wondered if they were the children of one of his colleagues.

He walked over to Liz, who had her phone to her ear. She hung up when she saw him.

"I was trying to call you."

"Amazing news, Liz. She's woken up."

"Who?"

"Kathy, of course. I spoke to a nurse."

"Is she talking?"

Jake said, "I don't know. I don't think so. But she's improving. Isn't that great?"

Liz sighed. "We need to talk. Urgently."

"Okay. Now?"

"Now would be best. But those gentlemen are here to see you."

Liz nodded towards the young men on the couch.

Jake whispered, "Who are they?"

"They're from LoveBugg."

"LoveBugg? What the hell is that?"

"The dating app."

A vague memory stirred within Jake. A phone call before Christmas. A Gary or a Gareth. He asked for a meeting, but was shy on details. They'd arranged a date and afterwards Jake forgot all about it. He supposed the appointment was in his diary, but he hadn't checked it.

Liz said, "The one who looks like he belongs in a 70s metal band is the CFO, Fran Duggan. The one who looks like a solider on leave is Gareth Reynolds, the CEO."

"They don't look old enough to run a lemonade stand."

"Find me after your meeting," Liz hissed. "It's extremely important."

"Okay, okay."

Jake walked over to the couch.

"Good morning," he said, extending his hand. "I'm Jake Whelan."

Gareth got to his feet and grasped Jake's hand. His grip was firm. A downy fuzz coated his upper lip.

"How's it going?" Gareth said. He had a quick smile and deep brown eyes. Perceptive eyes. "You forgot we were coming, didn't you?"

"Yes," Jake admitted. He was probably the only person in the building who would have said that. "I had no memory of it whatsoever."

Gareth laughed. "I like your candour."

He shook hands with Fran too. With his lean face and round glasses, he looked like the definition of a nerd.

"Come on," Jake said. "Let's see if a conference room is free."

The two young men followed behind, looking every bit like a couple of work experience students.

CHAPTER NINETEEN

At half past nine, Charlotte was walking past Conference Room 3 when she happened to see Jake and two young men through the glass wall.

She recognised Gareth Reynolds from LoveBugg at once. Charlotte knew the CEO of every significant company.

The second man looked familiar. Beneath his head-banger's hair, his face was thoughtful. He had the shrewd expression of a quant. Probably the company's finance whizz.

A quiver of excitement passed through Charlotte. A rumour was circulating – within a very exclusive circle – that LoveBugg had been offered a generous sum by one of the big tech companies, in return for a 49% stake in the company. This could be an excellent opportunity to get the work. Charlotte assumed that this must be an exploratory meeting.

She pushed open the door to the conference room.
Jake was saying, "Alright, let's begin."

It sounded like he was talking to himself rather than to the others. Charlotte saw right away that something had changed with Jake. He didn't look like the mess he had the previous day.

Charlotte cleared her throat. She said, "You weren't going to start without me, were you?"

The three men turned to Charlotte.

Gareth said, "I didn't realise we were having company."

He seemed annoyed to be interrupted, even by someone who looked as good as Charlotte.

Jake stood up. "Sorry, guys. Let me introduce you. Charlotte Flynn is head of mergers and acquisitions here. Would you like to join us, Charlotte?"

Gareth held up his hands in a *stop* gesture.

"No offence," he said. "But I figure finding one honest lawyer is rare enough. I don't want to push my luck."

Firm tone. Good insight. Impressive in someone so young, Charlotte thought. She let the door fall shut behind her.

"I work closely with Jake," Charlotte said. "I think you'll find my input valuable."

"We want to keep this between as few people as possible. We're talking about a sensitive matter."

Charlotte took her time, walking the length of the room. She stopped next to Gareth.

"Who made you the offer? Microsoft or Google? Or both?"

Gareth's head bounced back like he'd been punched.

"Where the hell did you get that?"

Charlotte smiled. "I heard about it weeks ago. I imagine they valued LoveBugg at about €125-175 million."

Now it was the turn of the long-haired man to look flummoxed.

He glowered at Charlotte. "The figures are confidential. Where did you hear that?"

"You must be Fran?"

"Yeah."

"I came up with the valuation myself. It's only an estimate, using a two-stage discounted cash flow model. I like to have a ballpark figure. Is the real number in that range?"

The two men exchanged a look.

Gareth gave a barely perceptible nod.

Fran sighed. He said, "€160 million. They told us not to tell anyone."

A surge of satisfaction washed over Charlotte, though she made sure not to let them see it.

Jake cleared his throat. "Charlotte is the best lawyer I've ever met. She knows what she's talking about, so I suggest you let her sit in and listen to her advice. Frankly it will be better than mine. Or anyone else's, for that matter."

"Fine," Gareth said. "You can stay."

Charlotte sat down. This deal could bring Grennan and Brennan huge fees, the kind that would make Arthur Grennan forget about firing Jake.

She soon had the measure of the two men. As expected, Gareth Reynolds was the visionary. Fran Duggan was the number-cruncher They were both a year out of college. The only surprise was that they had finished their degrees.

Charlotte took control of the meeting, both because she was better informed than Jake and to show Jake that she was the boss. She also wanted to establish herself as the face of the firm with LoveBugg. If things played out as Charlotte expected, she could be billing these guys for years.

As the meeting went on, Charlotte realised that Jake had built rapport with Gareth and Fran. They turned to him for confirmation of things Charlotte said. Though he barely gave a word of legal value, they believed he was a straight-shooter, and that could be valuable.

When the meeting was over, Charlotte and Jake rode down in the elevator with Gareth and Fran, and saw them to the door, where they shook hands and said their goodbyes. Charlotte was confident that she and Jake would get the work.

She was watching the two men walk away when Jake said, "I need to talk to Liz."

Charlotte was aware of Liz watching them. The receptionist looked like death, so clearly something was wrong. On the other hand, Jake seemed carefree.

Charlotte wondered if someone had found out about the hit-and-run. Maybe Jake didn't know yet. Or didn't care, for some reason.

Interesting.

Charlotte sensed two paths diverging.

"No," Charlotte said. "You can't talk to Liz. Come to my office. Now."

CHAPTER TWENTY

Charlotte's office was getting more cluttered, what with all the extra work she was taking on, but soon she'd clear it out. Charlotte hated clutter of any kind. Like Arthur, she believed in periodic pruning. Whether Jake would be pruned was still an open question.

She went and stood by her desk.

Jake followed her into the room.

"Close the door," Charlotte said.

He did, then turned to her. He said, "I forgot about the meeting. I would have told you if I remembered."

"Tell me what's happened," she said.

Jake shrugged. "What do you mean?"

"You seem less wretched today."

Jake's eyes lit up. "I found out that Kathy has regained consciousness."

"Lucky you," Charlotte said. Her leverage over Jake had been reduced, but not eliminated. "So what's up with Liz?"

"I don't know. I haven't had a chance to talk to her. You wouldn't let me."

"Don't blame me," Charlotte said. She crossed her arms. "I want you to draft a letter to LoveBugg in my name. Perhaps secretarial work is all you're good for."

Jake's face darkened, his hands tightened. He turned away from her and took a few steps toward the corner of her room. Then he shocked her by breaking out laughing.

Is it happening? Charlotte wondered. *Is he falling apart?*

"Well?" she said.

"I've just realised something."

"What's that?"

"If I don't take control of my life, someone else will be happy to. You or Liz or Grennan." He shook his head, then walked over to Charlotte. "Maybe it's time I decide for myself what I want to do."

Charlotte flinched as Jake stepped closer. He'd always been so predictable. Until now. He looked like he might strike her. Instead, he took Charlotte's face in his hands and kissed her. She was too surprised to pull away. His lips were softer than she would have expected. His fingers hot against her cheeks. She closed her eyes when he kissed her a second time.

Jake released her. He said, "I've wanted to do that since the first time we met."

Charlotte had too, but she didn't say so. She opened her eyes.

"What about Liz?"

Jake shook his head. "I should have ended things with her a long time ago."

There was a look in his eyes, something Charlotte saw the first time they met. A hint of the man Jake could become.

"I guess I'll go," Jake said.

"Wait."

This time, she kissed him, looping her arms around his neck and pulling his lips down to hers. She pulled away after a moment.

"I wanted this too," Charlotte said.

The door opened.

Liz stood in the doorway. Her eyes were wild. A furious howl ripped out of her mouth. She grabbed a book from Charlotte's shelf and threw it. Charlotte ducked as the book flew over her head.

"Slut," Liz screamed, then turned on her heel and stalked out of the room.

"Liz," Jake said.

Charlotte held his arm. "Let her go."

"I have to go after her. She's upset."

"Let her be upset," Charlotte said. "It's not going to kill her."

CHAPTER TWENTY-ONE

Liz fumed as her Honda sped down the road. She felt like driving into someone. Mowing down people on the footpath.

That evil slut.

She couldn't believe Charlotte had bewitched Jake. Her man. But men were weak, even the best of them, and Charlotte must have tricked him. Liz would wipe the smug smile off her face.

But first she needed to take care of something else.

Colin.

Lying dead in his apartment with a dishcloth down his throat. She had to destroy the evidence.

Liz stopped at a petrol station, where she filled a jerrycan with petrol. It would be obvious that it was arson, once the forensics people determined that petrol was involved, but so what? A good fire would destroy the evidence of her visit.

Colin had been a nasty piece of work and Liz was sure he had enemies. Who could predict where a murder investigation would lead?

Speaking of nasty pieces of work, Liz was going to make Charlotte pay for trying to steal Jake.

Tears rolled down Liz's cheek, blurring her vision. She'd never wipe that awful image from her mind. Jake and Charlotte standing in the middle of Charlotte's office, holding each other, kissing tenderly.

"Bitch," Liz screamed.

Her voice bounced around inside the car.

She reached her apartment building, grabbed the jerrycan of petrol, and hurried up to Colin's apartment. Many of their neighbours were away, visiting family over the Christmas break. She was relieved she met no one.

Colin lay in the kitchen where she'd left him. His face had lost its colour. Out of curiosity she touched his body and found it stiff and cold. Corpses were fascinating. Liz would have liked to observe what happened to Colin's body over the coming days, but she thought it was better to tidy things up here sooner rather than later.

She poured half the petrol over his head, and splashed the rest around the apartment, especially on the couch where she had sat the previous night.

Once she was satisfied, Liz threw a lit match on the floor in the kitchen, and another one in the sitting room.

The carpet caught fire with a fantastic *whoosh*.

When the fire was burning nicely, she stepped out into the corridor and closed the door behind her.

A man was approaching her from the end of the corridor. Vaguely familiar-looking. One of the men from last night. Colin's friend. Liz watched him, saw him look at her, his eyes tracking down to the jerrycan in her hand.

Liz turned and walked the other way, towards the fire escape. She forced herself to move slowly, calmly. To not look back until she was already at the end of the corridor. Then she couldn't resist. The man had just reached Colin's door. He was looking at it with his head cocked, and a puzzled expression.

Listening.

He didn't realise it was the fire he could hear. The man looked down, at the crack under the door, as the first wisps of smoke snaked out.

His eyes darted back to Liz.

Now he understood.

"Shit," Liz muttered.

She pushed through the fire door and ran down the stairs.

CHAPTER TWENTY-TWO

On the top floor, Jake made his way down the fluorescent-lit corridor to Arthur Grennan's office. He was giddy with excitement after what had happened in Charlotte's office. He'd surprised himself by kissing her, but the bigger surprise was that she had reciprocated.

He felt awful that Liz had seen them, but he would have had to break the news to her some time.

There was another difficult conversation he needed to have. Charlotte had said he was being paid less than other associates, despite all his years in the company. It sounded like Mr. Grennan didn't value him. Jake was now so far outside his comfort zone, he decided he might as well keep pushing.

Una Atkins, Mr. Grennan's secretary, was at her desk outside Grennan's office. She looked up when Jake approached. Una was so frosty, she always reminded Jake of a disapproving teacher he'd had when he was a kid. She was probably only ten years older than Jake, but she had one of those faces that belongs to a different era.

"I'd like to see Mr. Grennan."

Una reached for her diary.

"When?"

"Now."

A supercilious smile washed over her face.

"Mr. Grennan is not available today. I think he has an opening in the second week of January if that would suit you?"

Normally Jake would have turned and gone away, tail between his legs. Not now. He walked past Una, opened the door to Grennan's office and stepped inside.

The office was huge, stretching far to the left and right and enjoying spectacular views over the canal basin and surrounding area. It smelled like leather and aftershave.

The lighting here was more subdued than in the rest of the building. A large desk sat near the window. On the left side of the room, a cluster of three huge leather couches were grouped around a glass coffee table.

Mr. Grennan was perched on one couch, talking to Dermot Blake, the CEO of Ireland's largest bank. Blake's face was familiar from news reports, where he constantly seemed to be in trouble. He was almost as old as Grennan, but his thin grey hair was set in a fresher style than Grennan's and his face wasn't so stern.

All the same, Jake felt a sudden revulsion at the two men, sitting there like a couple of vampires, in their dark suits. Grennan gave Jake a cold look.

"What's this?"

"I'm sorry, Mr. Grennan," Una said. She nodded so deep it was almost a bow, and tugged Jake's arm. "I told him you were in a meeting."

"I want to talk about my salary," Jake said. Una's grip was like a vice. He turned to her. "Get your fucking hand off me or I'll sue the arse off you."

Dermot Blake broke out laughing. "He sounds like one of my traders, Arthur."

"I do apologise," Grennan said.

"You should be apologising to me," Jake said. He started walking towards the two men. "You waste years of my life, expect me to work every second of the day, pass me over for promotion again and again, and my salary is still…"

Jake paused. He was hyperventilating with excitement, and he had trouble finishing the sentence.

Arthur Grennan's scowl deepened. "I am having a discussion with Mr. Blake. Leave."

"You're having a discussion with me now."

Dermot Blake sat back in his chair, appearing genuinely amused.

Grennan shook his head. "Still what?" he said. "Your salary is still what?"

"Inadequate. I gave this company everything."

"Mr. Whelan, we don't want *everything*. We want results."

Jake shook his head. "I demand a better package."

"I'm not open to demands. If you don't find our compensation package satisfactory, you may go elsewhere. Goodbye."

"Come on," hissed Una, almost in Jake's ear.

"That's it?" Jake said. "I've worked here a decade and that's it? Then fuck you. I quit."

Even in the dim room, Jake could see Grennan's cheeks flush.

"Excuse me?"

"I'll write it up formally on a piece of toilet paper if you'd like."

Grennan got to his feet. His eyes blazed. "Mr. Whelan, how dare you?"

"I dare." Jake said, "I'd rather flip burgers than work in this kip."

"Bravo!" Dermot Blake clapped his hands together excitedly. He glanced at Grennan. "Sorry, Arthur, but I love a bit of gumption."

Jake turned and walked out the door. Una was right behind him.

What did I just do?

In the space of twenty minutes he'd lost both his girlfriend and his job. His life, as he knew it, was over.

Una closed the door, then put her hands on her hips. "Well, I never thought you had a spine."

Jake tried to think of a retort, until he saw her face. An expression that almost looked like admiration.

She said, "I've never seen anyone talk to Arthur like that."

"But I failed," Jake said miserably.

The secretary shrugged. "I don't know," she said. "Did you?"

CHAPTER TWENTY-THREE

Jake made his way back to the third floor. Friday, lunchtime, the building quiet. Anyone with any sense would be out enjoying life. And now Jake would be, too. He ran his hand along the wall as he walked, and he broke out laughing.

He thought of how surprised Mr. Grennan must have felt to have a staff member burst into his private office and interrupt him like that.

No wonder Dermot Blake had been so amused.

Jake could hardly believe he'd quit, but Fergal Long, the security guard, was waiting outside his office, and that made it real.

"Sorry," Fergal said. "I don't like doing this."

Jake nodded. "Not your fault."

Fergal sighed and started to read from a sheet of paper. "I have to inform you that Grennan and Brennan and/or you have terminated your employment with the firm. You are not required to serve your notice period. In fact, you are not permitted to so do. The firm requests that you vacate the premises with immediate effect, taking only your personal belongings. The firm requests that you not speak to any other member of staff. The firm would remind you of Section 4.1.A of your employment contract—"

"I get it," Jake said.

"I have to read it all. Sorry. I know it's a bunch of legalese bullshit. No offence."

"None taken." Jake said, "I'll pack up while you finish."

He went into his office and got his coat, emptied his personal things out of the drawer in his desk and stuffed them in the pockets of his coat. Hoping he wasn't forgetting anything, he made his way over to his desktop, so he could shut it down.

"Whoa, whoa, whoa," Fergal said. "They uh, they don't want you to access the firm's computer systems."

"Of course."

Jake stepped out of the room and turned to go to Charlotte's office. He needed to talk to her. Fergal blocked his path. He flashed an apologetic smile.

"Like I say, I really hate doing this. But I can't let you talk to other members of staff."

Jake didn't say anything this time. Shaking his head, he walked down the corridor. Fergal limped along behind him. The few people who were around watched as Jake was marched out of the building.

Fergal and Jake stood side by side, as the elevator carried them down.

"At times like this, I think of Seneca," Fergal said. "He said, 'Every new beginning comes from some other beginning's end.' Isn't that beautiful?"

Jake didn't answer. All he could think was that he wanted to see Charlotte.

When the door opened, they stepped out onto the deserted lobby. The reception desk was unmanned.

"Where's Liz?"

"Don't know," Fergal said. He held out his hand. Jake shook it. "Anyway, all the best, Jake."

"You too."

Jake stepped outside into the freezing December air. He started walking in the direction of the hospital. It might take him half an hour to walk there, maybe forty minutes, but he didn't mind.

In fact, he breathed easier with every step.

The anger he'd felt at Grennan began to ease. Maybe the old bastard wasn't so bad. Maybe he was actually right. No one had forced Jake to work there. If he didn't like it, he could have left years ago.

A car horn sounded nearby. Jake looked around to see a gleaming Jaguar pulled in at the side of the road.

Jake leaned down to peer in the front passenger window as it powered down.

"Well?" asked Charlotte.

"I quit," he said. "I told Grennan I'd rather flip burgers."

She smiled. "Get in."

Jake sat into the passenger seat. The car's interior was warm and smelled like vanilla. The news was on the radio, the volume low.

"How do you feel?" Charlotte said.

"Good question." Jake took stock of himself. "I feel… great. I was heading for the hospital. I wanted to tell Kathy the truth about what happened." Jake took a breath and let it out. "No more secrets. No more excuses."

"I'll go with you."

Charlotte launched the Jaguar back into traffic. She started to say something but Jake shushed her. An item on the news had caught his attention. A fire at an apartment building.

"Could you turn the volume up?" he said.

Charlotte tapped a button on the steering wheel and the radio got louder.

"Oh my god." Jake felt the colour draining from his face.

"What?" Charlotte said.

"Did you hear that?"

"Something about a fire?"

Jake said, "That's where Liz lives."

CHAPTER TWENTY-FOUR

Charlotte's eyes widened with understanding. A fire in Liz's building could be no coincidence. What had she done?

Jake hoped she hadn't hurt herself. If she did, it was on him.

"I need to find out what's happening," Jake said.

Charlotte changed direction at once.

They didn't talk. Jake couldn't have spoken even if he'd wanted to.

As the building came into view, he saw dozens of people standing around. The fire brigade had blocked the road off.

As soon as the car stopped, Jake flung open the door and hurried to the line of people standing looking up at one of the apartment blocks. Smoke billowed out of a cracked window on the floor above Liz's apartment.

Thank god.

It wasn't Liz.

The lady next to Jake was eighty years old if she was a day, and was dressed up like she was going out to the opera.

"Have you heard what happened?" Jake asked her.

"They haven't told us anything. It's probably a chip pan. Those things are lethal. Ooh, look at that."

Paramedics emerged from the lobby, carrying a body-bag on a stretcher.

Jake ran over to them.

"Is it a woman?" he asked.

"Out of the way," a fireman shouted.

"Man or woman?" Jake shouted back.

"A man. Now move back."

"Is anyone else hurt?"

The fireman shook his head as he hurried to the ambulance. Jake watched it go. He made his way back to the car, sat down in the passenger seat.

"It's not Liz."

Charlotte said nothing, just stared at the smoke billowing out of the building. Jake knew what she was thinking. It was still a hell of a coincidence.

"I should call her." Jake pulled out his phone. He dialled Liz's number and waited impatiently for her to answer.

Finally, Liz picked up.

"Are you okay?" Jake said. "I'm outside your building. I heard about the fire."

Liz said, "I can't believe you let that bitch... Anyway, never mind. Jake, I want you to answer a question truthfully. Do you love me?"

"Liz... I... this isn't the time for a relationship talk."

A long pause.

"Okay," she said. "We can talk later. Once I clean up this mess."

"What mess?"

"You know. All this stuff. Don't worry. I'll wipe the slate. Are you okay with using a different name?"

"What?"

"It's no big deal. After a week, you forget the old stuff anyway."

"What are you talking about? Where are you?"

"I'll call you later."

With that, Liz ended the call.

Charlotte looked at Jake. "What did she say?"

"I don't know what she was going on about. Something about starting a new life, and wiping the slate. Whether I'm okay with a new name."

"Jake, it sounds like she's in a dangerous frame of mind."

"You might be right. She wouldn't tell me where she is." Jake's stomach churned with fear. He had an idea. "Maybe her father can help. I mean, he can't speak, but he has an aide."

Charlotte shrugged. "I guess it's worth a try."

He brought up Google on his phone and looked up Grüne Felder, the Munich hospital where Liz's father was being cared for.

He found a number and called it. A man picked up after two rings.

"Hallo? Womit kann ich Ihnen behilflich sein?"

"I'm sorry. Do you speak English?"

"Yes. How can I help?"

"I'd like to speak to the aide who cares for Mr. Dubois, please. Mr. Christian Dubois."

"We don't have a resident by that name."

Jake felt a stab of irritation.

"You must know him. A French gentleman. He's paralysed. He has a daughter here in Ireland who video calls him every week."

"We have no French patients at all. Perhaps you have the wrong number."

"Is there another facility called Grüne Felder nearby? A second branch?"

"No, we only have one location. Hello? Are you still there?"

The phone fell out of Jake's hand.

Liz had lied to him.

Charlotte said, "What is it?"

"Her father is fictional. I think we need to get to the hospital. Fast."

Charlotte pulled away from the kerb with a screech.

CHAPTER TWENTY-FIVE

The supermarket across the road from St. Vincent's Hospital was always busy, but especially so at lunchtime. A lot of people were grabbing sandwiches to go, or taking the opportunity to do their grocery shopping during lunch hour.

Liz thought the self-service checkouts were her best bet.

She joined the queue, telling herself to be patient. Urgent as her business was, she couldn't afford to draw attention to herself.

Colin's friend had chased her down the corridor, and halfway down the stairs before giving up. If he hadn't seen her outside Colin's apartment as the fire started, she would have been fine. But he had to come along at exactly the wrong time. He must have been the one who called the fire brigade.

Liz had got away from there before they arrived, and had headed here to pick up a few things.

She tapped the back of the steak knife against her palm, irritated by the feel of the plastic cover. She wanted to rip it off.

In her other hand, she held a new meat tenderiser. The one she'd used on Colin had been so effective. It was a pity she hadn't brought it with her, but she'd forgotten. No harm, anyway. She'd found a new one easy enough, and she liked its heft.

Liz shuffled forwards, following those ahead of her as they moved gradually closer to the checkouts.

She really liked Jake.

She hoped he'd come around to her way of thinking. Starting over was easy, but Liz didn't want to do it alone. Her heart was set on Jake.

Only Jake.

No one was going to get in the way.

She got to the checkout and paid for her purchases.

Time for a visit to the hospital. Liz was going to make things easy for Jake and one day he would thank her.

CHAPTER TWENTY-SIX

Jake ran inside the hospital. He'd left Charlotte to park the car. There was no time to waste, if his fears were warranted. In the corridor, he ran into the nurse named Shilpa.

"Is Dr. O'Brien still here?"

"Yes, but—"

"Where? What ward?"

Shilpa pointed.

Jake didn't stop, couldn't stop.

He ran past the nurse and burst into the room.

It was a private room and Kathy was sitting up in her bed, supported by multiple cushions. The bedside table was covered with bouquets of flowers. A middle-aged man in a suit sat next to the bed with a notebook. He was taking notes while she talked. Jake let out a breath he hadn't realised he was holding.

"Kathy?"

"Jake? What are you doing here?"

He walked over and stopped beside her bed. "I'm so glad you're alright."

She smiled weakly before gesturing to the man at her side.

"This is Detective Tom Ryan," she said. "He's asking me about what happened."

Jake nodded a greeting to the plainclothes officer.

"Do you remember?" Jake asked.

Kathy frowned. "I was at home. I remember getting a call, but then… I'm not sure…"

"It was me," Jake said. "I called."

"Yes, seeing you reminds me."

The detective gave Jake a sharp look.

"What was it about?" Kathy asked.

Charlotte appeared in the doorway. She walked over, stopping a short distance from the bed.

Jake took a breath. He knew he would feel better once he had got the truth off his chest.

"I needed your help. I'd just been passed over for promotion at work."

Kathy gazed at him, her face blank. "I don't remember. They say it might take a while for my memory to return."

"You and I met in a café to talk. Then we walked outside. You got on your bike. That was when you got hit by the car. I was there. I saw it."

The detective leaned forward. His voice was low, gruff. "Why didn't you report this?"

"My girlfriend was the one who was driving." Jake glanced at Charlotte. "My ex-girlfriend."

"Her?" the detective said.

"No. The driver's name is Liz Dubois. She said Kathy was dead. She said we had to get out of there. I'm sorry I listened to her. I was an idiot."

Ryan said, "So that's who we saw on the CCTV. We have a team looking for that car."

Kathy touched the detective's wrist. "I'm sure it was an accident. Please don't be angry at Jake. I'm starting to remember." She closed her eyes for a moment. "I dropped something. Right? Then a car came out of nowhere."

"Yes," Jake said. "Only I'm starting to think it wasn't an accident. I've discovered that Liz has been lying to me. I'm not sure what's going on, but there's a fire in her apartment building."

Ryan cocked an eyebrow. "Now?"

"Yes. Maybe Liz wanted to knock down Kathy. I think she's dangerous. Her jealousy might be worse than I thought."

"People don't do hit-and-runs out of jealousy," Detective Ryan said. "Have you got any evidence of all this?"

"No. I'm worried Liz might be coming here. She was talking strangely. I think you need to protect Dr. O'Brien."

The detective stood up. He said, "You and I need to go down to the station. I want to take a statement from you."

"Sure," Jake said. "But you can't leave Kathy alone."

Her eyes widened. "Am I really in danger?"

"Don't worry," the detective said. "You're safe as can be."

The lights overhead flickered and died. Some kind of power outage? Jake met Charlotte's gaze and saw his fear reflected in her eyes. Kathy was far from safe.

Liz was already there.

CHAPTER TWENTY-SEVEN

The room was dark for a few moments before the backup generator kicked in. Its light was hardly strong enough to chase away the gloom of the winter afternoon.

"Never seen that before," the detective said, looking around.

Jake said, "There's more I need to tell you."

"Let me check with the hospital staff first. Check that everything is alright."

Jake saw Shilpa pass the doorway.

"I have a feeling everything is not alright," he said.

Ryan turned to Jake, the movement revealing the bulge of a handgun at his hip. He covered it again with his suit jacket. "What do you mean?"

"My girlfriend, my ex-girlfriend, I think she's dangerous. That fire—"

Ryan held up a hand. "Take a breath. You're talking about the woman who was driving the car when the accident happened?"

"Yes, but I'm sure it wasn't an accident."

Kathy sat up a little straighter in bed. "She hit me deliberately?"

"And I think she's here now. She wants to harm you."

"How do you know that?" the detective asked.

"I can't be sure," Jake said. "But I talked to her on the phone, and she sounded strange."

"I'm going to be right back," the detective said. His voice was low and stern. "And you and I are going to have a long talk about this. Down at the station."

"Okay," Jake said. "But please arrange for someone to come here to guard Kathy."

Ryan stalked out the door.

Charlotte said, "He thinks you're crazy."

"Maybe." Jake looked at Kathy. A cannula in the back of her hand hooked her into an IV bag of fluids at the side of the bed. "We're going to have to move you."

Kathy said, "Jake, are you sure?"

"If Liz finds you, I don't know what she'll do."

But he did know.

Murder her, Jake thought. *That's what Liz will do.*

"Let's hurry," Charlotte said.

"Take care of the IV bag."

Charlotte grabbed the metal stand while Jake pulled the bed away from the wall. He pushed it to the door, Charlotte keeping pace, and watching the IV line.

They moved out into the dim corridor. Jake saw Ryan's silhouette down the hall. The detective was talking on his mobile, paying no attention. Jake pushed the bed the other direction. They turned the next corner, down the hall to another ward.

Jake stopped in the doorway and looked inside. There were six patients in six beds. No nurses, no doctors. He nodded to Charlotte and they wheeled the bed inside. They pushed it to the far side of the room.

"I'll be back for you soon," Jake said. "You'll be safe here."

He patted her hand, alarmed to see that she was on the brink of tears. "It'll be okay," he promised.

He and Charlotte walked back the way they had come. When they reached the door of Kathy's previous ward, Jake stopped.

The detective lay on the floor. The handle of a knife stuck out of his belly and a meat tenderiser lay on the floor next to his head. Jake crouched down, and searched in vain for a pulse.

"Come in."

Liz was standing in the middle of the room, holding the detective's pistol.

CHAPTER TWENTY-EIGHT

Liz had a crazed look in her eye, and the gun in her hand did nothing to dispel that impression. Jake looked at the dead detective at his feet and then up at his girlfriend of a year. She stood about four metres away in the dim light of the backup generator.

"Where is she?" Liz said. "Where's Dr. O'Brien?"

"Doesn't matter," Jake said. "It's over."

"This place is over, this life. But we can start again. We can go somewhere new, *be* someone new."

"You killed a man."

A confused expression passed over Liz's face. "You mean him?" Liz used the gun to point at Ryan's body. "He got in our way. Everything I've done, I've done for us."

"I called your father's hospital. They've never heard of him."

"Sorry for fibbing. It was just a white lie. I had to make you stay with me. I needed time to show you we belong together."

"You lied about everything. The hit-and-run wasn't an accident, was it?"

Liz said, "I didn't plan it."

"How can you say we belong together?" Jake asked. "With no honesty, with no trust, with no love?"

"Of course, I love you," Liz said. That's why I'm doing this."

"And you'll even cut out the power in a hospital, even burn down an apartment building, to get what you want?"

Liz raised the gun and pointed it at Jake's chest. "We don't have time to debate it. Trust me, Jake. We'll start a new life together. Tell me where Dr. O'Brien is so we can be on our way."

The old Jake would have stood aside, told her where Kathy was and hoped for the best. But something had happened to Jake in the last twenty-four hours. He glanced at Charlotte. Only the tightness in her eyes betrayed her concern. Then he looked back at Liz.

"No," Jake said.

He took a step forward.

"Don't do anything stupid," Liz said, aiming the gun at his head.

Jake said, "All I've done is stupid things. But not anymore."

He took another step.

"Stop. I'll shoot."

"I thought you loved me."

"If you force me to shoot you, I'll do it."

Jake smiled. Despite the ferocious pounding of his heart, he suddenly felt free.

"Do what you want. I'll do what's right for me."

Liz gripped the pistol with two hands, steadying it.

Jake took another step closer.

He was almost within reach now. Was Liz willing to put a bullet in his brain? Jake had no idea. He closed more of the gap between them. Only a couple of feet separated them.

"Stop," she shouted. She swung the gun to the side, pointing it at Charlotte's head. "Stop or I'll blow that bitch's brains out."

Jake lunged forward.

He smacked the gun to the side. There was an explosion of heat and gas as the gun fired. A bullet blasted through a vase of flowers and blew a hole in the wall.

Jake shoved Liz backwards.

She tried to raise the gun, but Jake smacked it again and threw himself at her. The gun's barrel spun in the direction of the window and went off again.

Glass shattered and freezing December air rush into the room.

Liz hit Jake in the nose with the butt of the gun, knocking him to the floor. She turned the gun on him again and aimed it.

I'm going to die, Jake thought.

Then a glass vase arced through the air and hit Liz in the throat. It fell to the floor and shattered into smithereens at her feet. She gasped and dropped the gun.

Charlotte appeared next to Jake, looking like she didn't quite believe what she'd done.

Jake got to his feet.

So did Liz. They heard footsteps pounding the floor in the hall outside. Security staff, Jake hoped. There was no escape for Liz now.

She must have been thinking the same thing.

With a furious howl, she grabbed the gun off the floor and threw herself at the window, bringing her hands up to protect her face as she launched herself through the broken glass.

CHAPTER TWENTY-NINE

Dr. O'Brien's room was near the entrance to the Emergency Department, the window lying about ten feet above the ground. Liz was aware of that, as she launched herself into space, but she had no idea what exactly was beneath her.

Anyway, she had no choice. She wasn't going to let herself be arrested and put in prison.

Not again.

She fell into a row of bushes growing against the wall of the building. They were ferny and low, and did little to cushion her landing.

The impact winded her and knocked the gun out of her hand. But she scrambled to her feet and found she was alright.

She picked up the gun and looked around. There was no one about. Just sirens in the distance.

She'd done it.

She'd got away.

On her feet, she moved quickly away from the building, stopping at the edge of the footpath. She looked back and saw Jake and Charlotte looking out the window at her.

The sight of them together was enough to fill her with fresh rage.

She pointed the gun at them and squeezed the trigger once, twice, three times, until she had no bullets left. Charlotte and Jake ducked out of sight at the first shot.

Liz had no idea where the bullets went.

"You're dead," she screamed over the wail of sirens.

There was a lot to do. She had to create a new identity. She had to disappear and start again. She had to find someone new, someone who deserved her.

Before she went, she'd take her revenge on Jake and Charlotte. They weren't going to get away with this. For now, she had to run.

An ambulance shot up the road towards the Emergency Department.

"Liz," Jake shouted. "Wait."

She turned to see him leaning out the window, one arm stretched out as if he wanted to touch her. Tears of anger blurred her vision.

"It's not fair," she screamed, and stomped her foot on the ground.

"Liz!" Jake shouted again.

Distracted, she stumbled, tripped over her own feet.

She fell into the path of the ambulance.

It was moving too fast to stop, and Liz was off-balance.

She couldn't recover.

Would never recover.

The ambulance smashed into her. The last thing Liz heard was Jake's voice, still calling her name.

CHAPTER THIRTY

Two weeks later, Jake and Charlotte visited Kathy O'Brien at her home. The house was a comfortable semi-detached building, nestled in the middle of a housing estate close to the sea. Philip, Kathy's husband, gave Jake's hand a firm shake on the doorstep and led them into the kitchen.

Colourful children's drawings were stuck to the fridge. The whole family beamed out of snapshots framed on the wall.

They followed Philip through the kitchen to the conservatory, where Kathy sat in a padded futon, reading a Harlan Coben novel.

She looked up when they came in, and gave Jake a brilliant smile. She had been released from St. Vincent's the previous day. Jake gave her a hug and said, "You remember my girlfriend?"

It felt good to call Charlotte that, and for them to be there as a couple.

Jake had brought flowers. Charlotte, a get-well-soon card.

"Sit down," Kathy said.

Jake watched Philip as he took the flowers and went off to make tea.

"I thought your husband might take a swing at me," Jake whispered.

"Don't be silly. Philip doesn't blame you. Neither do I. You know that. By the way, I had another talk with the new detective, Thompson."

Jake nodded. Thompson was Ryan's replacement. Jake had met him at Ryan's funeral and spoken to him on two other occasions. He seemed like a decent man, though Jake couldn't say he'd enjoyed their talks together.

"We've spoken," Jake said.

"I reminded him that I bear you no hard feelings. I also reminded him of the stress you were under at the time of the incident and how you saved my life in the hospital. I hope they won't cause you too much trouble."

Charlotte squeezed Jake's hand.

"Even if they try," Charlotte said, "I'll make sure nothing comes of it."

Jake knew she meant it. She was willing to bring all her firepower to bear for him, if necessary.

Kathy pointed to a tabloid on the couch beside her.

"I don't usually read these rags, but, honestly, the things these journalists have found out about Liz…"

Jake nodded.

Liz Dubois wasn't actually her name and she had no paralysed father, no living family at all. But she had plenty of names, which Interpol was still trying to get straight. She'd been Kara Jansen while she lived in the Netherlands for three months, Bridget Bisset during eight months in Glasgow, Lisa-Anne Reich during a spring in Marseilles. A string of false IDs and violent incidents coincided with her relocations.

Jake hadn't begun to wrap his head around it.

While they chatted, Jake looked Kathy over. Every time he had visited her in hospital, she had perked up a little more, and now she almost looked normal, though a pair of crutches leaned against the side of the couch.

Brain damage had been Jake's main concern, but there was no indication that Kathy had suffered any, and, for that, Jake was grateful.

An hour passed quickly, and when the light began to fade, Jake and Charlotte excused themselves. Kathy saw them off from the doorstep. She said she needed to get up from her seat once in a while or she'd go crazy. Jake promised to visit again, some evening during the week. His new job would keep him busy during the daytime.

Jake had been surprised when Dermot Blake's secretary called him the previous week and asked him to hold for Mr. Blake. Jake had been even more surprised when the banker came on the line and offered him a position at the bank.

He'd accepted, though the position in the compliance department wasn't his ideal job. He'd have preferred to be a park ranger. But Blake had promised him he'd be dealing with land the bank had bought, so in any case there was a tenuous connection to the earth. Jake figured the work would be a change anyway, and a change was a step in the right direction. At least he'd have an income while he figured out what he really wanted to do. This time, the decision would be his. No one would make it for him.

As Jake and Charlotte walked down Kathy's driveway, Charlotte leaned in and kissed Jake on the cheek.

She said, "I want you all to myself for the weekend."

"You got it. Let's grab a pizza and catch up on Netflix. It can be a nice pizza, by the way. You've got that bonus to spend."

He was referring to the one Charlotte had received for her work on the LoveBugg deal. It had already made Grennan and Brennan a fortune.

"I'm not paying," Charlotte said. "Don't forget you owe me ten thousand."

Jake laughed.

"I thought you forgot about the bet."

"I never forget. Sometimes I forgive."

As they walked the rest of the way to the Jaguar, Jake realised that the old, familiar tightness in his chest hadn't bothered him for days, maybe a week. He took an easy breath, and squeezed Charlotte's hand.

"What?" she said.

Jake shook his head, because it was nothing, except that he was happy.

Printed in Great Britain
by Amazon